DEADLY AIM

BRENT closed his eyes and took a deep breath. His feet were planted firmly on the ground. His stance was perfect. His grip was solid. The room was cold.

He exhaled slowly and opened his eyes. He had a clear view of the target.

He stared down the barrel and took aim.

He squeezed the trigger.

He unloaded the entire clip on a rabbit as it rotated into sight.

A second later, the rabbit was gone. Only the bare stub of an armature completed its rotation.

Brent felt good. For the first time in days, in fact.

Suddenly, it all made sense. How he could correct all the wrongs that had been committed against so many. How he would use his newfound abilities to bring down Big Jack. No one would ever suspect it was him. It was the perfect disguise.

He would truly *bring justice to those who have none.*

Most especially, himself.

He'd spent the better part of a day down in the range. He'd gotten Worthington to retrieve a book on marksmanship and exhausted most of his supply of ammunition. He felt himself grow even stronger.

Only one question remained.

He'd never taken a man's life before, of course. This would be a lot different than rotating ducks made of tin.

There was every possibility that he'd have to shoot his target close up.

When the moment came, could he do it? Could he pull the trigger?

THE BLACK SPECTRE

BOOK TWO

NO VICTORY WITHOUT SCARS

BLACK HOOD PRESS

THE BLACK SPECTRE:
NO VICTORY WITHOUT SCARS
© 2017 Roger Alford

Published by Black Hood Press
An imprint of Lightning Bug Press
5535 Robinhood Village Drive, #103
Winston-Salem, NC 27106

www.blackhoodpress.com

First Print Edition: October 2018
ISBN-10: 1-949352-01-3
ISBN-13: 978-1-949352-01-6

Printed in the United States of America

10 9 8 7 6 5 4 3 2 1

PROLOGUE

Terminal City, 1886.

STATION MASTER EDGAR BUCHANAN stormed out of
the upstairs office of the Terminal City Depot and hurriedly
checked his pocket watch. Standing on the second-floor
landing, he leaned over the wooden railing and glanced
about the sprawling rail yard.

To the south he could see the stockyard off in the distance.
Most days you could smell it, too. It was the lifeblood of
Terminal City.

To the north he could see the few buildings and bridges
that made up downtown. Including the brand-new eight-
story Sherman Hotel.

With his eternally red face and sweaty brow, he always
looked on the verge of a heart attack. And with his dumpy
comportment, thick-rimmed glasses, and thinning hair, he
looked much older than his fifty-two years. Mrs. Buchanan
blamed the stress of the job. And his complete inability to
handle it.

The portly Station Master screwed his face into an angry
grimace and bellowed at the top of his raspy lungs. "Nate!
Nate!"

Dickie immediately stuck his head out the doorway of the
shipping office below and called back up. "Yessir?"

Dickie Smithson was reliable, punctual, and exceedingly
responsible. At twenty-three years of age, he was a devoted
husband to his young wife, Amelia. They already had two

children, with a third on the way.

"Dickie, has Nate come back with that box of time pieces yet?"

"Nosiree, not yet," Dickie chimed back. "I'd say he left here just a few minutes ago."

Buchanan checked his pocket watch again. He let out a low growl of frustration. Nate McGregor had caused him more than a few nights of lost sleep.

Despite being two years older than Dickie, Nate was the near polar opposite. He was unreliable, habitually late, and could rarely be depended upon for even the most menial of tasks. He spent half his days chatting up the engineers about where they were headed and the other half chatting up young Kitty Dawson down at her father's general store.

"I need that box," Buchanan growled. "It's due on the 4:30. If he's not back here in twenty minutes, I need you to run down there, got it?"

"Yessir!" Dickie sang out obediently.

"And tell him not to bother coming back!"

NATHANIEL McGREGOR strolled confidently into Dawson's General Store on Central Avenue. Though the large, wood-sided building was filled with shelves of dry goods, garden tools, animal feed, and just about everything else required of the modern household, his gaze searched for just one thing.

He made a beeline for the newly installed soda fountain where Dawson's lovely, dark-haired teenage daughter, Kitty, worked behind the counter. Though, to his thinking, she spent more time reading than mixing ginger ale or sarsaparilla.

She immediately called out to her father without even looking up from her pages. "Father! Mr. McGregor is here!"

Then she added quietly, "Finally."

"Tell him to wait right there!" Mr. Dawson shouted back.

Nate sauntered up to the counter. With his natural charm, manly good looks, and enticing Scottish brogue, he was very popular with a host of young women. Naturally, due to his rakish ways and vagabond lifestyle, he'd yet to settle down.

Born in Scotland, he'd found work on a merchant ship at age fourteen and made his way to America. He'd done the same with the railroads, intending to work his way to California. But, thus far, he'd only made it as far as Terminal City.

"Why hello, Mr. McGregor," Kitty greeted him cordially. She even took a moment to put down her book. "Can I interest you in anything else while you're here?"

Nate leaned over the counter with his wolfish grin and offered his usual response: "How about dinner to-night?"

"I was thinking perhaps something more like a cola. Or some caramels, perhaps?"

Undeterred, Nate launched into the latest version of his pitch, each one more grandiose than the last. "Actually, I was thinking we'd hop on the train over to Silverton. They have the finest steak dinner you'll ever eat at the Wyman Hotel. Then we'll head over to the Handlebars Saloon for drinks and dancing. What do you say, Lass?"

"But the last train from Silverton leaves at 9:00. How will we ever make it back on time?" she asked coyly.

"Well, if it gets too late," he replied, "we'll just stay over at the Wyman. Separate rooms, of course."

She gave him an incredulous look. "Come back in the morning? What kind of girl do you take me for, Mr. McGregor?"

Nate was not to be deterred. "Who says we have to come back? We could just take the train all the way to California."

"Thank you, no. Mr. McGregor," she stated firmly.

Nate stepped back in mock astonishment. "I promise you the night of your life, Lass. And all you can ever say is 'no, no, no.' Why is that?"

"In all the times you've attempted to sweep me off my feet, Mr. McGregor," she replied before returning to her chapter, "you've never once asked me what I'm reading."

"Well, I hate to break it to you, Lass," he cajoled her, "but I know the man you're looking for. Someone *down-to-earth*. Someone *devoted* and *dependable*."

She nodded in agreement.

"See, that's where you've made your mistake," he informed her. "Dickie is already taken. With a handful of kids to boot. I'm afraid I'm all you've got left."

"In this big city?" she asked with surprise. "Well, if the prospects are *that* bad, Mr. McGregor, I should get on that train myself and see where it takes *me*."

Mister Dawson came out of the back carrying a small crate of exquisite pocket watches. He showed Nate the contents before fastening the lid. "Twelve watches, all carefully repackaged."

Nate was surprised. "My, but these are the nicest watches I've ever seen."

"That's the problem," Dawson explained. "They're too expensive, and not what I ordered. With my overhead, I've got to charge twice what they cost. Nobody that shops here can afford a watch like this."

SEVERAL minutes later, as Nate reached the depot, he noticed a very well-to-do Gentleman waiting on the platform. He was an older fellow, with grey hair protruding from beneath his top hat and a belly that showed a man both well-fed and of means.

"Young man!" the Gentleman called out, shaking his pocket watch in frustration. "Would you be so good as to tell me the time?"

Nate looked down at the box he carried and sensed an opportunity. One that wasn't at all his to take. But was just too good to pass up.

"Good Sir, let me ask you this," Nate offered. "How much would you pay for a good, quality watch that always gives the correct time?"

"Young man," the Gentleman offered, "I'd be willing to pay a fair sum indeed."

And with that, Nate McGregor opened the small packing crate and soon made his first sale. Within minutes he had a very satisfied customer and a nice wad of cash in his hand.

There was just one problem, however. He didn't own the watches. Nor did he have the money to pay for them.

"Nate!" he heard Mr. Buchanan bellow overhead.

Make that two problems.

DICKIE SMITHSON was just about to make tracks for Dawson's General Store when Nate ducked in, breathless and excited.

"Well, thank goodness you finally showed up," Dickie exclaimed. "That box is due on the 4:30. I've got the paperwork and everything all ready."

"No can do, Lad," Nate replied excitedly. "Listen, I got an idea — "

Dickie instantly rolled his eyes. He'd long ago had his fill of Nate's hair-brained schemes. And he'd had to bail him out on plenty of them, too. But this time he'd have to draw the line. Especially with another youngster on the way.

"Forget it, Nate," Dickie interrupted. "Just bring it over here and let's ship that thing out."

Nate's sheepish grin told Dickie that he wasn't about to get the answer he wanted.

"But I already sold one."

AFTER dinner, Dickie's sweet, young wife, Amelia cleaned the dishes in their tiny, cramped kitchen. Their tenement in downtown Terminal City was barely big enough to house their growing family. But the rent was reasonable and it was close enough to the depot and the Dawson's General Store.

Nate followed Dickie into the equally cramped living room. He was ready to make his case. Nate moved Amelia's sewing basket as Dickie turned on the gas lamp.

"Don't move that too far," Dickie instructed him as they sat down on the threadbare furniture. "Amelia's got sewing to do after she gets the kids off to bed." With money as tight as it was, she managed to make a few extra dollars doing seamstress work at night.

"Just hear me out, Dickie," Nate pleaded before his friend could even state his objections. "I've been giving this a lot of thought — "

"Since this afternoon?" Dickie pointed out.

"Yes," Nate acknowledged, then continued in a low voice. "If I buy these watches, I can sell them meself and keep the profits! I cut out the middle man, see? And I don't have to worry about overhead!"

"No need to whisper," Dickie told him. "This place is so small, she can hear every word anyway. No secrets here."

"Right," Nate acknowledged, a little flummoxed but nonetheless undeterred.

"Okay, just for the sake of argument," Dickie countered, "how do you think you're going to sell them? You don't have a store."

"That's just it!" Nate explained. "I don't need a store! I just need a list of goods. I'll run ads in the paper. Not just here, but Kansas City and St. Louis. Then I can ship 'em out over the rails. Anywhere in the whole country!"

"Don't get ahead of yourself, now," Dickie chastised him.

The young family man scratched his chin and was surprised to find himself actually mulling it over. On the one hand, Nate McGregor was full of crazy ideas. In another day's time, he'd likely have yet another scheme cooked up and forgotten all about this one. But on the other hand, it *wasn't* a bad idea.

"All right," Dickie replied, leading up to the obvious question. "Where do you plan on getting the money?"

Nate gave him a sly, charming grin that he knew far too well. "I was thinking you could be a real pal and help me out."

Nate knew that while Dickie and his family lived hand-to-mouth, he saved every spare penny he could. Tucked away in coffee cans, the family Bible, and under their mattress was a tiny nest egg that just might be enough. He also knew that no one else would ever loan him the money.

Dickie knew full well that Nate never had a cent to his name. He lived every week from payday to payday. Helping him out *a little* actually meant helping him out *a lot*. Actually bankrolling the entire enterprise.

Dickie sat there silently for the longest time. He didn't even scratch his chin again, which Nate took as a bad sign. But he didn't outright say "no," either. Which was a good sign.

"I might consider it," Dickie finally responded. "But there'd have to be a lot of conditions."

"Like what?" Nate asked, doing his best to sound surprised that his pal would even suggest such a thing.

"First of all," Dickie explained, "we'd have to set up some kind of a finance plan. With regular cash payments. And interest of course. And penalties." He was doing his best to scare Nate off the whole idea. That was far preferable than trying to justify it to Amelia.

"Of course," Nate agreed, his enthusiasm dampened already.

"And then once you've paid back the money, assuming you actually do, of course," Dickie continued, "we'll need another plan for you to re-invest the profits. The last thing you want to do is go around spending any of the money you might actually make."

"I don't?" Nate asked, practically crestfallen by this point.

"No, of course not!" Dickie replied emphatically. "This is how you build security. Build your own nest egg. And after a few years of hard work and saving, you'll be ready to settle down and start your own family."

Nate just sat there quietly and finally muttered, "Right. Of course."

"You agree to those terms," Dickie emphasized, "promise on your mother's grave that you'll pay back every last nickel and accept the penalties if you don't, then I'll *think* about loaning you the money."

Nate stood up silently, ready to leave when Amelia waddled into the tiny room with her evening's work. "Not on your life, Nathaniel McGregor," she asserted.

She rubbed her stomach and picked up her sewing kit. "There won't be any such loan. If you want the money, it's a full and equal partnership. Fifty-fifty, right down the middle. Nothing less."

Dickie was even more surprised than Nate was. They both just stood there in stunned silence.

"Well," she finally had to ask, "are you two going to just stand there and gawk at each other? Or are you going to shake on it?"

Nate and Dickie happily grabbed each other by the hand. Both amazed to suddenly find themselves business partners.

"Well, what do you know about that?" Nate exclaimed happily. "McGregor & Smithson it is!"

CHAPTER ONE

Fifty Years Later.

OFFICER ROBERT SHAYNE sat by the third floor window of the Park Hotel on State Street. Tall, handsome, and clean-cut, a former military man who, in his dark blue uniform with shiny brass buttons, was the model of what a Terminal City police officer should be.

He took another drag from his cigarette as he watched the brick, two-story Quality Flour building across the street. From the outside it looked like a wholesome distributor. But anyone with any street smarts knew that this was where North Side Mob Boss Nails McCarthy ran his operations.

It was getting late in the afternoon and Shayne was ready for a break. He'd been staring out the window for hours, taking turns with three other flatfoots under the command of Detective Sergeant Michael Flynn.

Flynn was the near mirror opposite of Shayne. Dressed in a brown suit that looked a little too expensive for his weekly pay, he was thick around the middle and graying on top. A man who knew the city well and, thanks to his position, had found numerous ways to make it more comfortable.

Word on the street was that Whitey O'Leary was meeting up with Nails before skipping town. He'd been hiding out ever since gunning down two cops just a week earlier.

They'd had the whole city on lockdown ever since. Whitey was a wanted man of the worst kind.

Shayne stubbed out his cigarette on the window sill. He really needed to stretch his legs for a minute.

Just as he was about to get up, he glanced out the window again and happened to spot a man round the corner. The fellow in question was cloaked in the afternoon shadows. And with a wide-brimmed hat on his head, it was difficult to see the man's face.

Shayne watched silently as the fellow looked casually about, making sure the coast was clear.

"Hey Boss," Shayne called to Flynn, "I think we got something here."

"Whitey?" Flynn asked, rushing to the window.

"Not yet," Shayne answered, straining for a better look. And wishing he'd brought a pair of binoculars. "I'm guessing that's Mossy Egan."

Since the Mob wars of the last few months, the North Side gang had lost a lot of ground. And major players. For that reason, a number of low-ranking hoods had all gotten promotions. Also, for that reason, the police weren't as familiar with all the new faces.

Flynn stepped up to the window, pinching his smoke tightly. Just standing there, watching, set his teeth on edge. He hoped this was their chance to get evens.

"Heh-lo," Shayne added as two more men rounded the corner and looked about with Mossy.

"That him?" Flynn asked, leaning over Shayne's shoulder for a closer look.

"Can't say for sure," Shayne answered, craning to study every detail of the two suspects. Without getting their attention or falling out of the window.

"The short one's got to be Kid Yellow Newman," Shayne asserted. He'd encountered him many times over while walking the beat.

Kid Yellow had a well-known penchant for picking pockets. And had the arrest record to prove it. Despite the tell-tale limp, he also had a reputation for hightailing it at the first sign of trouble. Hence the nickname.

"The other guy," he added, "I just don't know. I mean, it *looks* like Whitey, but I just can't say for sure."

Same height, same build. And best he could tell, same hair color. Who else could it be?

They watched a moment longer as the two taller men ducked inside the building. Kid Yellow was left outside on watch. And was immediately distracted by a stray cat.

"That's gotta be him," Flynn stated emphatically. "Call down to the paddy wagon. Tell 'em were moving in."

Flynn stubbed out his own smoke on the sill and patted Shayne on the shoulder. "Good work, Bob. After to-day, you'll make Detective in no time."

DAILY CRUSADER reporter Vicky Rose was having an early dinner with her co-worker and new boyfriend, the lanky and studious Denny Morris. Denny worked in the paper's archives (affectionately known as "the morgue"), which fit his librarian-like personality.

For only their third date, Vicky had insisted on a booth at the nearby Cosmic Diner, which was all shiny surfaces and tile floors in its Art Deco interior. It wasn't that she had any affinity for the diner, other than it was very close to the office (so close that Frank usually stopped there for breakfast. And lunch). But primarily it was decidedly far-less romantic than the location of their first date, Vicedomini's, which was where couples usually went to propose.

Vicky knew full well (after Denny had defensively explained it), that the only reason he had chosen Vicedomini's was that his uncle was the Maitre'D. And for that reason he knew he could get a good table. And even a discount. All of which didn't make her insist on the Cosmic any less.

Either way, nothing could dampen the immense pride that Denny felt walking in with her on his arm.

It also didn't dampen Denny's efforts in constantly peppering her with questions regarding her family. Which unnerved her to no end. She wasn't about to introduce him to her father just yet. If ever.

Nor did her talking about an entirely different subject.

"So you never saw the Man in Black?"

"No, I didn't," he answered in frustration.

Vicky just couldn't shake the topic from her mind. She tried her best to recall, but the memories of her ordeal at the Asylum were too hazy. And considering who all was there, Denny was the only one with whom she felt comfortable discussing it.

"Well," she insisted for the umpteenth time, "someone asked me if I was okay and loosened the straps. You were still unconscious. You had to be."

Denny tried best as he could to lay the issue to rest. At least as far as he was concerned. "I promise you. I never saw anyone else. But that's not what I was asking."

"Then what were you asking?" she replied in confusion.

"About your father," he reminded her.

"Look, Denny," she admonished, rubbing her temples, "I told you, I'm not interested in a full-blown courtship here. This is just for laughs right now, nothing more."

"I know, I know," he countered. "I'm just trying to get to know you a little better. What's the harm in that?"

It was his sweet-natured innocence that got to her. She knew he wanted something more from their relationship and would take it in a heartbeat. But if they were going to do this, he had to be understanding and take it slow.

"I already told you all about my family," she relented. "My mother's a teacher, and so's my sister. My brother works at the bank."

"What about your father?"

"The less said, the better," Vicky quickly retorted, rubbing her head again.

He'd noticed she'd been doing that quite a bit lately. Ever since that night at the Asylum.

"Do you think I use the word *puerile* too much?" she inquired, quickly changing the subject yet again.

"I don't know," he replied, puzzled. "Why?"

"Somebody mentioned it recently, that's all." She opened her eyes wide and put both hands to her head.

"Another migraine?" He couldn't help but be concerned. Even if she found his concern a little too forward. Just like everything else.

"It's nothing," she brushed him off. "Just a little headache. I'll be fine. 'Course, working under Lyons doesn't help."

Though she'd successfully made it to the crime beat, City Editor Frank Matson hadn't quite trusted her yet to work on her own. So he'd assigned her to shadow a senior reporter, Chester Lyons.

"You were saying about your father?" Denny queried gingerly, trying to coax her back towards the topic at hand.

"Like I told you before, we don't exactly get along anymore. He thinks being a reporter is *unseemly*."

She let out a brief sigh, then suddenly became more candid. "Had one foot in the grave for as long as I can remember. I'm always worried one day I'll get a call from my mother that something's happened. And then it'll be too late."

Denny was about to ask "too late for what?" But then he realized what she meant.

He struggled for something comforting to say, when suddenly it no longer mattered.

"Hey Vick," the Waiter shouted, interrupting. "Frank just called. The cops just raided Nails McCarthy's office up on the North Side."

"POLICE! It's a raid! Hands in the air!" Shayne shouted, pistol at the ready.

He stormed the lobby. Right behind him was a gun-wielding Flynn. Plus five more men in blue, all armed with shotguns.

The phone rang just as they barreled inside.

It was large room on the second floor. The walls were beige and mostly unadorned, save for a large Quality Flour sign. There was a small reception desk and a row of filing cabinets to the left. On the far right was a partially open office door. The top half had an opaque window that read "Manager."

To the casual observer, it looked just like any other respectable business.

The first clue to the contrary were the four Irish toughs standing around the reception desk and having a smoke. They quickly put their hands up, very surprised.

"Where's Whitey?" Flynn barked as the phone rang again. No one answered.

The cops quickly surrounded the group and Shayne frisked them for weapons. The two officers immediately recognized three of them as the men they'd seen down on the street. Kid Yellow, Mossy Egan, and... a fellow named Spike Kinney.

Who clearly wasn't Whitey O'Leary. But he sure looked like him from a distance.

The fourth ruffian was a red-headed bruiser named Cockeye Dunne. Who, of course, wasn't Whitey, either.

Damn.

Flynn rushed to the office door and was met by Dapper Sheridan, Nails' new right-hand man.

"Say, what's the idea?" Dapper snapped as the phone rang again behind him.

There was no mistaking him, either. With his bowler hat, three-piece suit, and finely trimmed moustache, he always looked like he'd just stepped out of the men's clothing pages of the Smithson & Gregor catalog.

"Where's Whitey?" Flynn demanded as he shoved his pistol into the young mobster's face.

"No idea," Dapper sputtered before Shayne grabbed him by the collar and shoved him toward the others.

"Get them out of here!" he commanded. "Arrest the lot of them!"

Inside the office, Jimmy "Nails" McCarthy stood beside a large, oak desk with his hands held high. His coat was on the chair and his suspenders the only thing over his shirt.

Shayne frisked him carefully as the phone rang one last time.

The office was just as plain as the lobby, except much smaller and with three open windows along the outside wall.

"Where's Whitey?" Flynn demanded again. He jabbed at Nails with his sidearm.

Nails just stood there — defiant.

That wasn't good enough. Shayne slugged Nails hard across the jaw. Then once more in the gut to make his point.

Nails doubled over for a second or two, but remained

silent. Then he stood back up and looked Shayne straight in the eye. Defiant as ever. They didn't call him "Nails" for nothing.

"Don't make me ask you again," Flynn instructed. "There's a lot more where that come from."

Nails just stared back at him angrily. Then he finally responded through gritted teeth. "Don't know what you're talking about, Copper. Ain't seen him for weeks."

As Flynn paced angrily about, Shayne noticed that something on the desk had gotten Nails' attention.

"Don't toy with me, Jimmy," Flynn warned him angrily. "Word on the street is Whitey's been holding up and is meeting you here to-night. So you tell me! Where is that cop-killing bastard?"

Nails stayed silent.

Flynn slugged Nails himself just for good measure.

As Flynn turned around, Nails quickly grabbed a scrap of paper from the desk and shoved it in his mouth.

"He's trying to swallow something!" Shayne alerted. He quickly grabbed Nails by the jaw, but the Irish ganglord held tough and refused to spit it out.

Shayne drove three solid punches straight into his gut. Nails coughed and gagged, but still refused.

Flynn hit his breaking point. "You think you're tough, do ya?" he shouted in Nails' ear.

He pressed his pistol against the right side of Nails' chest and pulled the trigger.

As Nails winced in horrible pain, he finally spun around and opened his mouth. The paper fell out onto the floor.

Then Flynn shot him twice more. First in the neck, and again in the back.

Nails finally crumbled to the floor, screaming in agony.

"Ain't so tough now, are you boy?" Flynn shouted angrily.

Shayne just stood there in stunned silence.

"Pick that up, will ya?" Flynn asked as he shrugged in resignation. Then he raised his pistol to his own arm and pulled the trigger.

The round just barely grazed him. But it was enough to rip through his jacket and cause him to bleed.

Moments later, Flynn made for the office door, clutching

his injured arm.

"I been shot!" he cried out.

Completely stunned, Shayne watched as Flynn barreled down the stairs and shouted, "Quick! Call an ambulance!"

WHITEY O'LEARY stepped out of the telephone booth and let out a sigh of deep concern. He'd tried to warn them, but was obviously too late. There'd been no answer.

"Any luck, Whitey?" Squint Mulligan asked.

"No," Whitey replied, as they both turned and looked down the block. The paddy wagon was parked outside the Quality Flour building. They had stood and watched as Flynn, Shayne, and the other cops had charged inside.

By a sheer stroke of luck, he and Squint had been just a few minutes late for the meeting with Nails. For him, that was like missing the Titanic and a sure date with destiny.

"Come on, let's get out of here," Whitey instructed. "This place'll be crawling with cops in no time."

"But what about the money?" Squint asked.

"Forget it," Whitey answered. "We'll just have to figure something else out."

WHEN Vicky Rose arrived at the crime scene, she was surprised to see the paddy wagon and two police cars driving away. She'd gotten there too late as well.

She'd had to drive all the way over from downtown. Had she and Denny gone back to Vicedomini's like he'd suggested, she'd have been a lot closer.

And just when she'd finally made the crime beat and really needed to prove that she she could cut it. *Great work, Vick*, she thought.

She looked around for Chester Lyons, but it appeared he'd already gone, too. Couldn't say she was disappointed.

The only vehicles still there were an ambulance and the coroner's car. Waiting by the ambulance was a white-haired Irish Priest, smoking a cigarette with a young Rookie cop.

So, she reasoned, there was one person later than her. Nails McCarthy. And he was getting ready for a one-way trip to the Morgue. The real one.

But the absolute icing on the cake was that *Terminal*

City Standard reporters Charlie Hecht and Ben Gelbart had also beaten her there. No surprise, since every other reporter in town had done the same. Those two may have been second-rate, but they clearly had better contacts.

Naturally, they were the first ones to greet her. With all the smarm they could muster, of course.

"You're too late, Doll Face," Charlie heckled, while still managing to give her his usual once-over. "Missed the whole thing."

"Must've been out getting her hair done," Gelbart chuckled, throwing a quick elbow Charlie's way.

"So, any chance you mugs want to fill me in on what happened?" Vicky asked. She tried to sound sincere but was unable to mask the disdain in her voice. "Help a girl out?"

"Normally, we don't make it a habit of assisting the competition," Charlie began, checking her over once more. "But what kind of gentlemen would we be if we didn't aid a fair damsel in distress?"

His lascivious grin made her want to punch him right in the kisser. But that wouldn't have gotten her the information she needed.

"Would you?" she asked, smiling through clenched teeth as she opened her notebook.

Charlie straightened his tie, then gave her the scoop. "Detective Sergeant Michael Flynn, that's with two Ns, killed Nails McCarthy and even took a bullet himself!"

"Wait, Nails McCarthy is dead?" Vicky reacted with surprise. *Make that the third surprise in less than five minutes*, she thought. So, that's who was headed to the Morgue. All the flower shops in town were about to get really busy.

"Yeah," Gelbart added. "Detective Flynn's a true hero! City needs more cops like him."

"That's right," Charlie bragged. "We're on our way to the hospital right now to get an exclusive with Flynn. See ya there, Doll Face!"

They chuckled to themselves as they jumped in Charlie's car and drove off. Hats off to them.

Vicky stood there in shocked disbelief. Not just for barely

missing out on a major scoop, but for what Nails' death meant for the city. With Whitey still on the lamb, there'd be nothing stopping Big Jack and the South Side mob from taking over now.

Vicky was about to follow the boys to the hospital, when she realized maybe that wasn't the best idea. Every other reporter in town had that angle covered. Instinct told her to stick around. And instinct was about to pay off in spades.

Not even five minutes had passed before the ambulance drivers carried out Nails' body on a stretcher. He was covered in a sheet that was deeply stained with blood.

They were followed by a tall, clean-cut cop. She'd seen him around. Thought his name was Shayne, but she wasn't sure. Might have even read about him in the paper once before.

He'd already loosened his tie and took a big step back when they reached the meat wagon. His hands were bloody, and he didn't seem to notice. He seemed pretty frazzled by the whole situation.

Big guy like that? Surely this wasn't his first stiff. Now that would have been a *real* surprise.

But that was nothing compared to the biggest shock of all. In a night of surprises, this one took the Triple Crown.

The Priest threw away his smoke and knelt down to perform last rites.

He crossed himself and said a prayer, then reacted with a start.

After a moment of stunned silence, he cautiously lowered his head to the corpse's chest. Then he quickly straightened right back up.

"This man lives!"

CHAPTER TWO

VICKY watched as the Priest hurriedly pulled back the blood-soaked sheet from Nails' face. He was most definitely alive, but barely.

"You must get this man to a hospital!" the Priest exclaimed.

Shayne just stood there, momentarily stunned. His face was a mix of relief and confusion.

Finally, he barked to the Ambulance Drivers, "You heard him! Get him to the hospital! Hurry!"

The men quickly loaded Nails into the vehicle and shut the doors. Shayne dashed off to his own car down the street.

Not such bad luck after all, eh Vick? she thought. But before she got too full of herself, she needed to know where they were going.

Luckily, she managed to stop a Driver just before he got behind the wheel. "Which hospital?" she asked.

He shook his head and replied, "Bridewell Prison."

"Wait, why aren't they taking him to the emergency room?" she asked, thoroughly confused.

"We don't take these guys to a hospital. Don't you know anything?" he scoffed before slamming the door and speeding off.

BIG JACK TORRISIMO raised his wine class and offered a hearty toast to his men.

Since the shootout at the Belmont two weeks earlier

(during which, only Willie Potatoes Binaggio had taken a bullet), they'd claimed much of the North Side as their own. Whitey O'Leary was on the run from the Cops. And Nails McCarthy had just met his end.

They had a lot to celebrate.

To cap off this victory, Big Jack was about to open his latest venue, the Four Diamonds. He treated the small crew to a lavish feast in the upstairs dining room. There was food, wine, and cigars aplenty. And the company of a bevy of beautiful women awaited them afterwards.

On the outside, the club was unobtrusive and looked like any other office building. But on the inside, it was Big Jack's most lavish yet. Ornate, custom wallpaper with pineapples in the design, mahogany woodwork and trim, and lush red carpets on every floor. On the ground level was a saloon and cafe for dining, dancing, and the finest in entertainment. The second and third floors had large rooms for private parties and gambling. And the top floor had plenty of smaller rooms for his girls to entertain his best customers.

"I'm glad to have all of you here to-night," Big Jack began. "We got a lot to celebrate. I wanted you boys to be the first to enjoy the hospitality of this new establishment before our grand opening next week."

"Salute!" the men cheered and raised their glasses in appreciation. With one arm still in a sling, Willie Potatoes dropped his cigar and toasted with the other.

"And most of all," Big Jack concluded, "I want to offer a toast to our old friend Nails McCarthy. May he Rest In Peace."

"Salute!" the men cheered again.

They'd recently expanded the inner ranks to include a few new faces. Young Tommy Auferio, who'd barely survived a previous shootout thanks to his aversion to raw clams. Frankie "Eggs" Milano, cousin of Spats' previous driver Paulie Milano (may he Rest in Peace). And Dominick "Fingers" Scarrone, who, thanks to his itchy trigger finger, had saved Spats' life at the Belmont.

Willie Potatoes offered his own toast. "To Big Jack! A

man so smart, he actually got the cops to do his dirty work!"

"Hey," Big Jack replied, "just doing what the Mayor says. Helping to clean up the city!"

"Salute!"

"Hey, Spats!" Willie Potatoes called out. "How about passing Tommy the clams!"

"Yeah, very funny, Willie," Tommy replied. "But those clams saved my life!"

As a result, his previous nickname of "Little Tommy" had quickly given way to "Tommy Clams." As much as he hated being called after a dish he despised, there was no fighting it. He'd carry that moniker for the rest of his short life.

Eggs Milano lit up a cigar and studied the decor. He noted that, in addition to all the pineapples in the wallpaper, they were also carved into the mahogany woodwork. There was even a ceramic one on the mantle.

The doors opened and Big Jack's young mistress, Estelle Mercer, sashayed inside. She was young and vivacious, with her blonde hair cut into a fashionable short bob. But what appealed to Jack the most was her genteel Southern accent. Courtesy of her well-to-do upbringing in Savannah, Georgia.

She was followed by several more girls from the club, each as beautiful and tempting as the last. The men let out a low howl of approval as they quickly picked their favorites and paired up.

"Spats, I got to ask you," Eggs inquired after nuzzling with a young brunette. "If the place is called the Four Diamonds, what's with all the pineapples?"

Eggs was sure he'd royally stepped in it when Spats immediately turned towards Big Jack and loudly relayed the question. "Jack, Eggs here wants to know why all the pineapples?"

Eggs quickly demurred, but it was too late. He studied Big Jack's expression, but saw nothing but a smile. *Surely, the Boss wouldn't do anything in front of all these girls*, he thought.

Big Jack tugged Estelle by the hand and led her over to the young muscle. "Why don't you explain it to him, Dear?"

"Of course, Darling," Estelle replied cordially. "You see,

the pineapple is the symbol of hospitality. There's an old tradition that you put one on the mantle to welcome your guests."

She pointed out the ceramic pineapple over the fireplace. "Then when you're ready for them to leave, you just take if down. All very politely, of course."

Willie Potatoes joked as he pretended to lob a grenade. "Hey, the same thing's true in Terminal City. Except, here we just toss it through a window!"

VICKY followed the ambulance to the back of Bridewell Prison. She watched from her car as Shayne and the Ambulance Drivers unloaded Nails and rushed him inside on a gurney. She'd been vaguely aware that Bridewell had its own medical facility. Though she was pretty sure they were hardly equipped to treat a man with three bullets in him.

She followed them in close behind. It was a small lobby area that still looked more like a prison. The walls were plain beige, the reception desk behind glass, and the double doors to the facility itself were securely locked and controlled by the guards.

Luckily, no one paid any attention to her, which had already proven to be a major benefit being a gal reporter. So, she graciously took a seat in the tiny waiting area and watched.

The doors opened and the young prison physician, Dr. Fettes, with thinning blond hair and a permanently harried expression, rushed out to examine his new patient. He was closely followed by Nurse Evans, a middle-aged negro woman.

"Thank you, men. We'll take it from here," Dr. Fettes instructed the men. Then they went back out to the ambulance.

Nails was already ghostly white by this point. The young doctor just shook his head as he did a quick evaluation.

"Think he stands a chance, Doc?" Shayne asked, hopefully.

"In a hospital, maybe," Dr. Fettes replied. "But not here. It's a miracle he's still alive. But I'm afraid we're looking at a lost cause. We can give him something for the pain, at least."

Nails let out a low groan. He weakly lifted a bloody hand and pawed at the Doctor's coat as the guard opened the doors.

He struggled to speak and finally managed to get something out. "Call... my... lawyer."

"He doesn't need a lawyer, he needs a priest," Nurse Evans commented as they wheeled him back. The doors shut automatically behind them.

Vicky rubbed her temples and watched inconspicuously as Shayne just paced nervously about. It looked like he was completely overwhelmed by the whole situation. He stopped and eyed the phone on the wall, then went back to his pacing.

Chances were, she reasoned, he needed to let his superiors know about the change in situation. Chances were also good, however, that it would all be moot very shortly.

Vicky desperately needed to ask him some questions. Especially to get his take on what had happened. At that moment, she only had the word of Hecht and Gelbart. Which, in her mind, was practically worthless. But still better than nothing.

And she was there alone with one of the only witnesses. This was an unbelievable chance, but her head was killing her.

She also needed to call her editor, Frank Matson, and let him know what was going on. She was sure he had no idea that Nails was still alive. If only momentarily. Luckily, there was a pay phone on the wall, but talking to Shayne was her top priority.

But she also knew, then, that she'd have to play her cards very carefully if she was going to get any kind of statement.

Instead of going to talk to him, however, she breezed right past and made a beeline for the powder room.

It was tiny, all tile, with barely enough space for one person. She went ahead and locked the door, even though she was certain to be the only woman there.

She grabbed a pill bottle out of her purse and, cupping some water from the miniature sink, quickly downed two more of the horse pills prescribed by her doctor. The water had a strange taste, but with her headache returning she didn't much care and stomached it anyway.

So many things had changed since the Asylum. She'd been suffering from splitting headaches for starters. Her memories of that night were fuzzy at best, just flashes really. The Basement Lab. Dr. Hyneman. Ned Vogel. Vito Spats. And despite what Denny said, she actually did remember someone else there. A man. Dressed in black. Who might have helped them. She wasn't sure.

But Denny never saw him. Probably just an orderly. Or her mixed-up imagination.

That's what Frank said, too. Especially after what they did to her.

GUS KONRATH made sure Nurse Evans was still at her post. Then when she wasn't looking, slipped around the corner and down the prison hallway.

As a guard at Bridewell, he was working the medical unit when Nails McCarthy was wheeled in. It didn't take a genius to know that he wasn't supposed to be alive.

Konrath peered back down the hallway to make sure no one watched. He figured with all the commotion going on, all eyes would be on Nails. He figured right.

He ducked into Dr. Fettes' office and made a beeline for the desk. He quickly picked up the phone and dialed.

Konrath tapped the desk nervously as it rang. He was beginning to think no one would answer. Then finally he heard a young voice on the other end. Sounded like a real shindig going on in the background.

"Hey, who is this?" Tommy Clams asked, clearly annoyed. "This better be important."

Konrath didn't have time for pleasantries. "Let me speak to Spats," he barked back. "This is Konrath down at Bridewell. Tell him it's urgent."

CHESTER LYONS lit up a smoke and shoved his way through the throng of reporters that filled the Emergency Room at Terminal City General. The room was all dark suits and cameras instead of the usual white walls and tile floors. Seemed like every other reporter in town and beyond was there. Any complainers (and there were a few) got a burn on the arm.

Lyons was an old-school news hound who lived off of booze, cigarettes, and the thrill of chasing down a good story. His second wife had left him years earlier, so he just spent most of his time (free or otherwise) hanging out at O'Doule's Bar. And since he knew just about every copper in town, this was where he got his best leads.

He forced his way up to the front, right next to Charlie Hecht and Ben Gelbart. As much as he liked those younger guys, he wasn't about to let them beat him to a scoop.

"Say Charlie, any sign of the Doc?" Lyons asked.

"What'dya say, Chester?" Charlie greeted him with a slap on the back. "We was wondering about you. Where's your secretary? She get lost?"

"I could be so lucky," Lyons grumbled. "Probably out getting her nails done."

When Frank assigned Vicky to shadow him, Lyons took the news even worse than she did. He knew he wasn't getting any younger and didn't like the idea of grooming his own replacement. Especially a woman.

"You're not sending me to City Hall, Matson!" Lyons had barked loud enough for Denny to hear down in the basement. "I'll drop dead first!"

"Just goes to show you," Gelbart added. "Crime beat's no place for a skirt. Can't even find her way to the story when you tell her where to go."

As much as he agreed with the first part, Charlie well knew Vicky was smarter than that.

"I don't know," Charlie commented. "Something smells fishy to me. Ain't like her to not be here."

Before he could give her tardiness another second's thought, the surgeon stepped out and the crowd of reporters erupted in a barrage of questions.

"Speaking of dames," remarked Gelbart. Much to everyone's surprise, it was a *woman doctor*. Not bad looking, even for one in her early 40s.

Lyons said what all of them were thinking when he added, "I'll be damned."

After she'd held up her hand for a long stretch and repeatedly asked for the pack to quiet down, they finally did just that.

"Good evening, gentlemen, I'm Doctor Carol Nelson, the attending surgeon for Detective Sergeant Michael Flynn."

Before she could continue, there was another barrage of questions, accompanied by the blinding light and cacophony of flash bulbs.

Doctor Nelson raised her hand again and was eventually able to continue.

"Is he gonna live, Doc?" Lyons blurted out.

"I'm happy to report that Detective Flynn received only a superficial wound to the lower part of his left upper arm," she continued. "He will not be able to use the arm for awhile, but we anticipate that he will be discharged soon and make a full and speedy recovery."

"You hear that boys?" Charlie shouted before she could even finish. "Detective Flynn is a hero!"

The throng of reporters erupted in a barrage of cheers and a hundred more shouted questions. *How long will he be out? Did you save the bullet? Did he loose a lot of blood?*

Lyons forced his way back through the crowd, determined to get to a phone. He had his headline and he was hell-bent to be the first to get it in.

VITO SPATS wasn't at all happy about leaving the dinner. He was just on his way upstairs when Tommy told him about the phone call. But quickly changed his tune when he heard what it was about. He told the girl to go upstairs and wait for him then followed Tommy to Big Jack's office.

"What?" Spats shouted over the phone in disbelief.

"I swear to you, Spats," Konrath told him. "I seen him when they come in. "Shot up like hell, but still kicking."

"You're sure he's still alive?" the underboss asked.

"Sure as I'm standing here," Konrath confirmed. "Doc doesn't think he'll pull through, but I thought you oughta know."

"You just make sure when he leaves, it's in a body bag," Spats ordered.

He slammed down the phone and stopped short of hurling

it across the room. "Unbelievable! Flynn put three slugs in him. How can he still be alive?"

"That Mick bastard's tougher than we thought," Willie commented.

"Yeah, well Cherry Nose took seven, and he's still recovering," Spats replied. It was quickly becoming apparent to Spats that he'd never make it upstairs. None of them would.

"So much for letting the cops do our dirty work."

VICKY returned from the powder room relieved to find Shayne still there. She knew she hadn't been gone that long and likely could have caught him in the parking lot. But still, she would have royally kicked herself had she missed the opportunity.

Which she was just about to do when a well-dressed, but rough-around-the-edges, gray-haired, bearded Irishman stormed into the lobby. He practically knocked Vicky over as he barreled straight towards Shayne.

"Get me the physician in charge! Right away!" he demanded.

"And who are you?" Shayne snapped back.

"*Doctor* Albert Reilly," he commanded, as if his title alone should have carried thunderous weight. "I'm James McCarthy's *personal* physician."

Vicky had to stop and think for a second about whom he was talking. Then she quickly remembered he meant Nails.

Apparently, she surmised, the Mob boss had gotten his phone call.

Shayne returned momentarily with Doctor Fettes. Reilly wasted no time in making his demands. "Why on God's green earth is this man not in a hospital?"

"Doctor, you know it's standard policy that anyone charged with a crime comes here," the young prison doctor countered. "They *don't* go to the hospital."

"Well, I'm having him transferred," Reilly insisted.

"On who's authority?"

"Mine!" Reilly commanded.

Fettes threw up his hands in surrender. "Okay, he

probably won't survive it. But we'll have him prepped and ready in a few minutes."

"See that you do," Reilly commanded before storming out. "I'll have my operating room ready and waiting when he arrives."

Fettes turned to Shayne and remarked, "Looks like this is going to be a long night for you."

"And then some," Shayne replied.

GUS KONRATH checked the hallway once more before ducking back into Dr. Fettes' office. He raced for the phone and nervously dialed the number. The only thing worse than delivering bad news was waiting too long and dealing with the repercussions later.

He didn't even have to wait for the phone to ring this time. And he didn't have to wait for Tommy to get anyone, either. Spats picked it up himself.

"So, Spats," Konrath said nervously. "Afraid I got some more bad news."

SHAYNE was nearly out the door when Vicky stopped him.

"Officer Shayne?" she asked softly.

"Yeah?" he replied, puzzled. He'd barely noticed she was there.

Judging by the exasperated look on his face, she'd figured the soft approach would be the better way to go. And judging by his responses, she'd figured right.

"I'm so sorry to bother you," she began, "but I was wondering if you could answer a few questions. I'm Vicky Rose, with the *Daily Crusader*."

That last bit took him aback. He'd wondered when the press would show up. Hadn't expected that they'd been there the whole time.

His instinct would have been to kick her out right on her keister. But he hadn't expected a dame reporter, either. Especially one looking like that. One bright spot in a very unpleasant evening.

"You don't say, huh?" he replied. "Well, this has been a night for the books."

Vicky pulled out her notepad. "I just wanted to get your

take on the shootout. Just to get a better idea of what occurred."

His demeanor suddenly changed. "Look, it happened just like Flynn said. Word for word. We went in, McCarthy pulled a gun, and took a shot at us. Hit Detective Flynn in the arm."

He demonstrated the location of Flynn's injury, then continued. "Detective Flynn returned fire and struck McCarthy three times. In the neck, the right side of his chest, and the lower back."

Vicky scribbled furiously to get it all down. "What kind of a gun was it?"

"Excuse me?" Shayne asked, clearly not expecting the question.

"The gun," she repeated. "What kind of gun did Nails have?"

"Oh, it was a..." Shayne hesitated. "Actually, I don't remember. You'll have to check the police report."

"Of course," Vicky replied. Though she was puzzled by his inability to answer.

She was about to ask another question, but the doors opened and Dr. Fettes came rushing back in. "Officer, we're just about ready. We'll have him back out any moment."

"But Officer Shayne..." she began.

Too late. He didn't stop to listen.

BIG JACK sat back in his office chair and contemplated the disappointing news. He'd called a quick end to the celebration and ordered Spats and Willie into his office. Eggs, Tommy, and Fingers were sent outside to stand guard. Just in case.

Big Jack hadn't survived this long by running off half-cocked at the first sign of trouble. His response would be careful and measured. Just like always.

"Where'd this doctor take him?" Big Jack asked.

"Konrath says they're headed to Terminal City General," Willie replied. "We got people there. We can make sure he don't make it to morning."

Big Jack inhaled deeply and twisted the diamond ring on his right hand. "No," Big Jack answered. "I want you to stay away from this thing. Nails got the message loud and clear. He knows the drill. We don't got to worry about him no more."

In his older years, Big Jack had grown more tolerant of loose ends. But not Spats.

"What about Whitey?" Big Jack asked. "Any word?"

Spats answered through gritted teeth. "Never showed. Cops got there before he arrived."

Willie's natural instinct was to punctuate it with an expletive, but he knew when to keep his mouth shut.

"Spats, I need you to find him," Big Jack commanded. "If the cops knew where he was, theyd've taken him out already. If he's still in the city, somebody'll talk."

"You got it, Boss," Spats assured him.

"But don't rattle any cages just yet," Jack added. "Give it a few days to let this whole Nails business get off the front page.

Just as Spats had expected. Time to clean up the mess. Again.

And now he was supposed to take his own sweet time about it.

Big Jack twisted his ring a moment longer and finally grumbled. "I don't know much about this copper Shayne, though. What do you hear?"

"Think he was in the paper a few years ago," Spats replied. "Made himself a hero."

"Yeah," Willie confirmed. "Saved some kids or something. Might've even taken a bullet."

"I need Willie to go talk to him," Big Jack instructed. "Make sure everything's square. That he's a standup guy. And anybody else you think we should worry about."

"Sure thing, Jack," Spats agreed.

But his face easily belied his words.

VICKY hightailed it down the highway and screeched to a stop at the first phone booth she saw. After what she'd just witnessed, she didn't want to call from the prison. Luckily, there was a gas station less than a mile away and they had a booth on the corner.

She was short on change, so she checked her watch and

gambled that Frank would still be at the office. She dropped in her nickel and quickly dialed the number.

"Red?" he barked. "Where in the hell have you been?" No John-Brown-its this time. She knew she was in trouble. "Every other paper is at the hospital getting the lowdown on Flynn!"

"Yeah, well they don't know the *real* story! Nails is still alive!" she snapped back.

Frank went suddenly quiet. For a moment she thought the line had gone dead. But it was really just the sound of Frank being stunned into silence.

"Wait? You mean Nails is *alive*?" he stuttered. "Where'd you hear this?"

"Hear nothing," she told him. "Saw it with my own eyes. They took him down to Bridewell. But that ain't the half of it."

Frank knew a major scoop when he heard one. With ink in his veins, he could smell one from a mile away.

"Okay, how soon can you get here?" he asked.

"Better to meet somewhere else," she told him. "Some place where the walls don't have ears."

OFFICER SHAYNE grabbed a stool in the bar at McGillin's Tavern, a restaurant and watering hole in his North Side neighborhood. A dividing wall of natural wood separated the upscale dining area from the narrow bar on the opposite side. They were as much known for their soda bread and Irish stew as their Guinness and whiskey.

It had been one hell of a night. As much as he wanted to get home to his beloved wife and son, he really needed a drink first.

Most of the other cops liked to frequent O'Doule's. It was a decent enough place, but the press liked to hang out there, too. Always on hand for a scoop. And anyway, he much preferred to be alone when he drank.

As expected for a week night, the crowd was pretty thin. The only other person at the bar was a well-dressed young woman at the other end. Shayne didn't know much about ladies's garments, but she looked a little old-fashioned, despite her obvious youth. Might have even smiled at him, but he was too deep in thought to notice.

The bartender, Sam, was rather surprised to see Shayne darken his establishment. Especially in an unofficial capacity. "What's doing, Bob?" Sam asked. "Don't see you in here too often."

"Give me a whiskey," Shayne sighed.

"Tough day at the office?" Sam asked with a half smile as he poured a shot glass.

"Yeah, you could say that," Shayne tried to smile, then tossed it back. He slid the glass right back to Sam. Nodded for him to go ahead and refill it.

"Tell you what," Sam offered. "Why don't you go clean up? And I'll have another one right here. Waiting for you when you get back. On the house."

"What?" Shayne asked, completely puzzled.

Sam gave a nod and Shayne looked down. He finally saw the blood on his hands.

CHAPTER THREE

BIG JACK watched curiously as Vito Spats poured himself a Scotch. He swirled it around in the glass a moment or two before finally taking a swig. Spats was never much of a drinker. It was a quality that had served him well during the boom years of Prohibition.

"Something on your mind, Spats?" Jack finally asked.

The room was empty save for the two of them. Willie had been dispatched to get the car. And Frankie Eggs, Tommy Clams, and Fingers Scarrone were all still outside standing guard.

"I'm just concerned about this Nails business," Spats explained. He looked around cautiously to make sure the two of them were still alone. "No disrespect, but I was just thinking. If you'd let me take care of this before like I wanted, we wouldn't be in this mess."

"Careful what you say, Spats," Big Jack warned him. "You just remember who's boss, got it?"

Spats fumed to himself. He'd have to do a better job of hiding his dissatisfaction. So he quickly changed the subject. "Sorry, Jack. Of course."

"Listen," Big Jack explained. "If anyone goes sniffing around, I want the cops to take all the heat."

"But what if one of 'em spills?" Spats asked.

"You do what I told you and they won't," Jack explained.

"But what if they do?" Spats asked, wondering how Jack could be so sure.

"Then we'll take care of it," Jack told him. "Don't worry, I got an ace up my sleeve."

"Right," Spats agreed, forcing a chuckle. Big Jack had been talking about that ace for years. But never once had he let on what it was. Spats didn't like being left in the dark. By Jack or anybody else.

"Sometimes I wonder if it's even real," he smiled.

"Oh, it's real," Jack smiled back. "And one day I'll tell you. But until then, just like I said. I don't want you to get anywhere near this thing. Capiche?"

"Yeah, I got it," Spats assured him. But he still wasn't happy about it.

VICKY sat on the couch in Frank's living room and listened intently as his twin daughters, Audrey and Lillian, performed on the flute and violin, respectively. Frank's lovely wife, Betty, conducted as her girls delicately moved through both a Beethoven sonata and "Turkey in the Straw."

Vicky had called just as they were sitting down for dinner. She'd gotten there right at the tail end and Betty had graciously fixed her a plate.

As a hard-line newsman, Frank's house was the opposite of what she had expected in every way. The wallpaper was dainty with floral designs, every chair and sofa had a doily, and every room had a distinctly feminine touch. Anyone who visited would be hard pressed to find evidence that Frank even lived there.

Vicky absolutely adored Betty. She was shapely, dark-haired, and always wore the most lovely dresses. Kind of reminded her of her sister. And Betty's manners were impeccable. She could easily have taught Emily Post a thing or two. Frank was tame as a kitten around her. No wonder he tried to stop swearing.

As a schoolteacher married to a newspaper editor, she and Vicky had a lot in common and had immediately bonded over war stories. And just like her own sister, Betty was whip smart and completely involved in Frank's work. Vicky loved how there were no secrets between them.

"Brava!" Betty applauded when the girls completed their final duet. Vicky did the same, though with a bit less enthusiasm. Not because of the girls, but because it made her sound like her own mother.

"That was wonderful! Upstairs now girls," Betty instructed as she got up. The twins gave everyone kisses and said their good-nights. Again, it reminded Vicky so much of her own childhood. It was clear Betty ruled her house with a firm hand.

"I'll be back in a few minutes," she whispered as she led the girls out.

THE LONG BLACK touring car pulled up to the Mercantile Exchange Building on Union Street. Built just six years earlier, the forty-five story Art Deco structure was the tallest in Terminal City. The outside was sheathed in Indiana limestone. Ten stories up above the entrance was a grand, 13-foot clock which could be seen for blocks. It was flanked by two hooded, stone figures: one holding corn and the other wheat. In addition to its many tenants, it was primarily home to the Board of Trade, where livestock and grain futures were bartered daily.

But most importantly, it also held the offices of Cosmopolitan Holdings. One of the largest conglomerates in the city, Cosmopolitan had interests in stock futures, real estate, steel mills, building construction, stage and screen entertainment, and the import of fine Italian wines.

Fingers Scarrone and Frankie Eggs both got out of the driver's seat and checked around. In the best part of town and well within South side territory, this was known to be an extremely secure area. But they could never be too careful. Especially with both Big Jack and Spats in tow.

With the coast clear, they opened the back doors and escorted the two capos into the building. This was Eggs's first trip and he couldn't help but marvel at the three-story lobby. Everywhere he looked in the perfectly symmetrical interior he saw shiny, black and white marble. Except for the glowing white rectangular light fixtures that hung from above. And the thirty-foot tall naked statue of Ceres, the Roman goddess of agriculture, grain, and fertility. Frankie Eggs finally had to let out an impressed whistle for that one.

A quick ride up one of the 23 elevators took them to the 38th floor. And to the sleek and modern offices of Cosmopolitan. The furniture was modern and dark leather. The walls ornate with Art Deco patterns. Soon they were in the office of the company president, where Fingers and Eggs stood watch at the door.

Spats offered the man a firm and friendly handshake. But Big Jack greeted their host like a brother, with a vigorous hug that signified both respect and adoration. "Buonasera, Sal! È bello vederti!"

Salvatore Crocetti was tall and thin. With his receding black hair, finely tailored suit, and genteel manner, he looked every inch the respectable businessman. Years earlier, back in the days of Prohibition, Crocetti had been a partner of Big Jack. But while Jack was determined to have virtually all of Terminal City under his control, Crocetti kept out of sight. He preferred to remain silent.

Over the years, he made many legitimate investments, most of which paid off handsomely. Yet, he still maintained an interest in Big Jack's endeavors, and had fronted most of the money for the new club. But always from a safe distance.

Crocetti was determined to bring respectability to his family. His sons had all adopted American names, such as James, Ralph, and Matthew, and worked for their father. Each one in legitimate business. But his greatest pride of all was his youngest. His beautiful daughter, Louisa.

"Buonasera, Giuseppe, Vito. Benvenuti! Per favore, siediti," Crocetti instructed.

With pleasantries aside, the three men sat down and Crocetti's expression quickly changed to one of deep concern. He took his investments very seriously. Most especially those managed by Big Jack.

"Capisco che le cose non stanno andando bene," he intoned with a furrowed brow. *I understand that things are not going well.*

VICKY and Frank both leaned forward in their chairs, careful not to raise their voices. It was finally time to talk business. To Vicky it felt odd to discuss such vulgar matters in such polite surroundings. But it was still far preferable than going back to the office.

"Three shots at close range," Vicky began, still in disbelief. "Can't believe he's still alive." Then she filled Frank in on all the gory details, though with less flourish than usual.

"Don't forget," Frank reminded her, "Cherry Nose Caifano took seven, and from what I hear, he's still hanging in there."

"Guess that's why they call him *Nails*," she concluded. "Probably use that in the headline."

"Come on, Red," Frank protested. "Nails getting gunned down isn't exactly a bad thing here. He had it coming in more ways to Sunday."

"Yeah," she replied, "but something about this one smells fishy to me. When I asked about the gun, Shayne couldn't tell me. What kind of cop doesn't know which weapon a perp was carrying?"

"Not any cop I know," Frank agreed. "Especially one who's been wearing a badge as long as this Shayne has. Might have something there, Red."

"Think maybe Nails wasn't carrying?" she pondered. "But if he wasn't, then how did Flynn get shot? And what were the Cops doing there in the first place?"

Vicky could feel her headache coming back. She rubbed her temples and lied back on the couch. "Something's screwy about this whole thing. And I want to find out what it is."

"How's the patient, Dr. Freud?" Betty asked as she came back in.

Another woman might have been suspicious at the sight. And let jealousy get the better of her. But not Betty. She'd already offered Vicky something for her headache as soon as she'd arrived.

Betty commented, "Well, I think it's pretty clear that the police in this city are just as corrupt as the criminals they're tasked to apprehend. If not more so."

Vicky rubbed her head again. This one was coming back with a vengeance.

"Told you the crime beat was no place for a woman. You got what you wanted, Red," Frank shook his head. "How does it taste?"

"Like penicillin," she answered.

"Franklin Ronald Matson," Betty admonished him. "You could at least try to be a little more sympathetic." The firm hand wasn't just for the girls.

Frank quickly apologized. Well, *that* was something Vicky never heard at the paper.

"You need a glass of water?" Betty asked her.

"No, I took two down at the prison," Vicky demurred. "I take any more, you'll have to put me up for the night."

"Well, if you change your mind, just let me know," Betty offered.

Vicky put on a brave front. "Nothing I can't handle, believe me. Doc says they should pass in time."

"Listen, Red," Frank implored, as much for Betty's benefit as for Vicky's. "There's no telling what that quack down at the Asylum did to you."

"Well, whatever it was," Vicky answered, "it was worth it to save an innocent man's life."

"You just be more careful on this one, Red," Frank told her. "I've a feeling this could run pretty deep."

Vicky sat back up and closed her eyes for a moment.

"Well, somebody's got to do something about this corrupt city. I mean, who can we depend on? The courts? The police? They're all on Big Jack's payroll. But if even just one person speaks out, fights back, maybe others will want to stand up, too."

"We'll do the best we can, Red," Frank agreed. "But just remember, that's what Thomas Gregor thought, too."

CHAPTER FOUR

BRENT GREGOR sat in the back of his rented touring car at the Los Angeles Municipal Airfield. He watched through the curtained window as the crowd outside stood and cheered. He was happier than he had been in many years.

Off in the distant sky, a small plane approached the runway. It was a single engine aircraft with slightly tilted wings. Brand new and being developed for the military as a fighter.

Its pilot was Abigail Wentworth. And after a total flying time of 14 hours and 55 minutes, she was about to become the second woman pilot to take home the Bendix Trophy. And set a new record in doing so.

Naturally, Brent had followed the race in the papers even since before the pilots left New York. He was determined to be there when she landed.

Now that he could finally walk again, he'd come to win her back. There was nothing left to keep him trapped on the ground while she soared to greater and greater heights. He'd no longer have to stay behind. Her victory would only make their reunion that much sweeter.

Of course, there was the small problem of her current suitor. That newspaper publisher, George Parkhurst, whom he'd actually met in India. And had to be a good ten years older than her. Plus he was new money and from what Brent had seen and read, very much an opportunist. He was really more of a promoter than a fiancé. Certainly not the kind of man she'd want to marry. Otherwise, she would have married him already.

The race had not been without worry. There had already been two near-fatal accidents. But, with luck and prayer, all of the flyers survived.

The first occurred when pilot Jim Howard's plane just spontaneously exploded mid-air over Kansas. By some miracle, he was actually thrown clear by the blast and parachuted to safety.

The second was when husband and wife team, Ben and Maxine Jacobson, crashed in New Mexico on a Navajo Indian reservation. The Navajos who witnessed the accident had a terrible fear of death, so the pair lay trapped in the wreckage for over two hours before help was able to arrive.

Watching her plane get closer and closer brought back a flood of memories. Some very good. Others he'd forever like to forget.

He pulled the curtain shut. "Take me back to the hotel. Would you, Worthington?"

"Don't you wish to stay and congratulate her, Sir?" Worthington asked.

"Not here. Not now," Brent replied.

"Of course, Sir," Worthington complied.

As they drove off, Brent couldn't help but think of their college days. She'd helped him to make other friends, so after Stephen's death, his fellow students would readily help him get to class. Worthington had eventually relented when he protested the idea of hiring another student.

On the plus side, she no longer made him promise to be nice. Abbie had routinely gotten on him about treating others "like they're servants" (particularly Stephen). He never fully agreed with that assessment, but had complied nonetheless.

At some point, however, he began to see less and less of her. He couldn't exactly put his finger on when. But he was dead certain he knew why.

His inability to walk, he felt, had started to come between them. He feared that she had found someone else. Someone who wouldn't keep her grounded. Someone who ignited her passions enough to make her forget all about him.

He'd only been half right. She surprised him in the library one afternoon. He was studying at a table, and she plopped down across from him. It'd been days since he'd seen her. He couldn't remember the last time she'd snuck into his dormitory room.

"Hey Big Spender, how's tricks?" she asked with a mischievous smile.

She sounded more like a character in a movie and not at all like herself. Brent got the sudden feeling that she was hiding something. Or was about to share bad news.

That feeling was only bolstered when she reached over and kissed him. It was clearly an afterthought, something to disguise the fact that anything was amiss.

All of this was followed by a long, awkward silence. This was something they hadn't really experienced since childhood.

Brent started to respond but then stumbled on just what to say. He was still new at building interpersonal relationships. This was one of those moments where he typically depended on Abbie. And in this instance, she clearly wasn't helping.

He was perceptive, however. And this much he knew. Something, or someone, had clearly come between them.

"I haven't seen you since last week," he finally told her.

"I know," she replied, trying to sound like nothing was wrong. "I've just been so busy. Has it really been a week? Oh, my heavens, I didn't realize."

More long silence followed. Accompanied by the drumming of her fingers on the table.

Finally, she leaned in close and whispered. "Look, there's something I need to tell you." She nervously pulled her hair behind one ear in that way that always made him sit up and take notice.

"What is it?" he asked defensively, fearing the worst. Even with his extremely limited experience with courtships, he was reasonably sure she'd come to break it off.

Which only made what she said next that much more surprising. "Can you meet me in front of the dormitory at 3:00? I'll come pick you up."

He just stared back in puzzled silence. *Why would she*

need to pick him up? He wondered. Despite the need to keep their voices down, she still could have done it right then. There was no need to prolong the inevitable.

"Why can't you just tell me?" he had to ask in frustration.

"You'll see," she told him with a sly smile as she got up. That last action completely threw him off.

She glanced back at him through a lock of hair that fell over one eye.

He had no idea of what to expect.

AT PROMPTLY 3:00, Abbie pulled her two-door convertible up to Brent's dormitory. She'd changed from her school uniform of dark blue skirt and white cotton blouse to, shockingly enough, a pair of khaki men's pants and light blue shirt.

"What on earth are you wearing?" he asked. "You look like a highwayman. You'll get ten demerits if anyone sees you."

"It's for the surprise," she answered. "And we won't be here that long."

She helped him get in the car, which was really just maneuvering his wheelchair into the right spot so that he could easily lift himself in. Since there was no way to fit the chair in her automobile, she wheeled it back inside.

It was fortunate for both of them that Abbie had a car at Emerson. It was even more fortunate that she'd learned how to drive. Her mother had never learned how, nor did many of the women of Lakeview Heights. Brent's own mother included. But Abbie had shown so much curiosity as a young teenager, Mr. Peterson, the family chauffeur, had given her lessons. By the time her father had raised any objections, she was already driving all over the estate.

Where he did firmly put his foot down was when she'd asked to drive all the way to Emerson on her own. No amount of childlike pleading could get him to budge on that one. Where he finally conceded was to allow her to take the train and have Mr. Peterson drive the car to Emerson for her. Afterwards, of course, Peterson took the train back.

"Where are we going?" he asked as she climbed into the front seat.

"You'll see," she answered again with an excited smile.

She put the car into gear and quickly sped through the winding campus streets and out the back way. They sat in awkward silence as she drove several miles down a long wooded road. Brent tried multiple times to start a conversation, but he only had one question on his mind. And it was one that she adamantly refused to answer.

Her continual response was the same sly smile and the words, "You'll see."

She eventually turned down a dirt road and finally arrived at a small, makeshift airfield. She parked near a dilapidated wooden barn, around which were a handful of red and yellow biplanes.

"What's this?" he asked in confusion. "Are we going to watch the planes?"

"Something like that," she told him.

Abbie leaped out of the car as a young pilot stepped out from around a yellow two-seater biplane. He was rough and tumble and ruggedly handsome. Very different from Brent in every way. And much greater competition than Brent could have hoped.

The pilot immediately called out to her. "Abbie!"

Clearly, she had been there many times before.

For just a moment, Brent was worried that this was the young suitor whom he imagined had stolen her affections. But then just as quickly he put the thought out of his mind. Abbie would never be so cruel as to take him there to meet his rival.

She immediately turned to Brent and said, "You have to promise not to tell anyone about this. Not Billy. Not my parents. Not even Worthington."

Brent thought that was an odd request. They already had several secrets between them. Besides Worthington, he couldn't imagine telling anyone in her family. He rarely saw her older brother, Billy. And her parents lived in London.

Rather than debate the point (which was his natural instinct), he just did as she asked. It was something he had learned well in the course of their relationship. "I promise."

What instantly made him feel even better was her

introduction. "Joe, this is my boyfriend, Brent."

No obfuscation. No hesitation.

Joe immediately reached out for a handshake. But before he could say a word, Abbie exploded with bottled excitement.

"Joe's been teaching me to fly!"

Brent had never seen her so enthusiastic. She took a moment to gather herself. But only a moment.

"Father would be so appalled if he knew! He once made Billy promise to never get in an aeroplane. That's why I've been keeping it a secret. But he never made me promise. As you can see."

Brent was vaguely aware of Billy's agreement never to fly. Mr. Wentworth had gone to an aerial stunt show and witnessed a crash that nearly took out an entire group of onlookers. As soon as he'd gotten home, he summoned young Billy and made him swear to "never set foot in one of those infernal things."

But since Abbie was a girl, and a few years younger at that, Mr. Wentworth never thought to make her take the same oath. Had he known what was in store, he might have sworn her off driving, too.

"Great to meet you, Brent," Joe finally shook his hand. "Abbie's told me so much about you."

Brent stumbled on what to say in return. He, on the other hand, was at quite the disadvantage.

"Sorry, Brent," Abbie apologized. "But I've been wanting to surprise you. And not tell my parents, of course."

"To-day's her big day," Joe informed him proudly. "First solo flight."

"Yes!" She grabbed him excitedly. "And I want you to come with me!"

Brent sat there in stunned silence. This day had certainly been full of surprises. First at finally learning what had been going on. And second at the thought of riding in an aeroplane. With Abbie alone at the stick.

"You're not afraid, are you?" she implored. "Will you? Please?"

Looking into her eyes, how could he be? She'd already given him so much strength.

"Yes, yes, of course," he replied anxiously. Then immediately tried not to think about his decision.

He sat in the car and watched as Abbie put on her flying gear (which, he had to admit, was rather fetching) of hat, scarf, and goggles. Then they checked the plane over and eventually proclaimed it ready for takeoff.

As Brent wondered how on earth they would get him in that contraption, Abbie ran back to the car.

"You're not going to chicken out on me, are you?"

Brent denied it. While privately wishing that he could.

Joe called for another pilot and the two men handily picked Brent up on their shoulders as if in a victory celebration. Once they got to the plane, Brent lifted himself into position and dropped down into the rear passenger seat. Abbie climbed up to buckle him in. Getting back out would be another matter. Which meant that he was stuck there until they landed.

With Brent securely fastened, Abbie crawled into the cockpit (now a misnomer if there ever was one, Brent thought) on her own and gave him an excited kiss.

"You ready?" she asked excitedly as she handed him his own goggles.

She strapped herself into the pilot seat and checked her controls. She and Joe gave each other a thumbs up. Then Joe turned the propeller and quickly stepped back.

Brent felt his heart sink into his stomach as the engine roared to life. Within minutes the contraption started to move.

Abbie turned the bi-plane towards the dirt runway and maneuvered into position. Brent felt his heart sink as they were about to take off.

She stopped momentarily and turned around. Then shouted something to him as she gunned the engine.

He couldn't hear a word she said. But it didn't matter. The excitement on her face told him all that he needed to know.

Abbie had found her one, true love.

CHAPTER FIVE

ABIGAIL WENTWORTH entered the famous Cocoanut Grove at the Ambassador Hotel to thunderous applause. The orchestra immediately began playing "Off We Go Into the Wild Blue Yonder," which added a chorus of laughter and more applause.

Her suitor, George Parkhurst, was soon at her side with an enormous bouquet of white roses. As he took her in his arms, they turned towards the crowd and were bathed in the glow of a thousand flashbulbs.

She needed a moment to adjust to her surroundings. Even as someone who'd grown up surrounded by the opulence of Lakeview Heights, this was a world unfamiliar. The vast nightclub was ornate and tropical. With its painted ceiling and artificial palms, it felt just like a movie set. And everywhere she looked she saw famous faces, many of whom she'd only seen on the big screen.

On the outside, she fit right in. None could have ever guessed that just hours earlier she had been cramped in a tiny cockpit piloting her way across the country on her own. But with her cultured upbringing, short bobbed hair, and silk evening gown, she fit right in. The faint scar was only barely visible on her neck. George had assumed it was from a flying accident. She'd never told him the truth.

That she looked every inch the movie star had not been lost on him. As a newspaper publisher who'd clawed his own way up on talent, handsome looks, and perseverance, he'd set up this soirée to introduce her to all the power players of Hollywood. If Sonja Hennie could be a movie star, he reasoned, so could Abbie.

One reporter shouted, "Miss Wentworth! Any truth to the rumors that you might do a picture?"

"Oh no, not for me," she told him. "I'm only interested in flying."

Parkhurst immediately jumped in and added, "But you never know. Anything can happen in Hollywood!"

"Wealthy and beautiful girl pilot makes her triumphant debut." That would be the next morning's lead story in *Variety*, *The Hollywood Reporter*, and a host of other papers. Even one from her hometown.

As someone who'd longed to escape the gilded artifice of her upbringing, the world of Hollywood held little appeal. She only wanted to fly. To be up in the clouds, where she felt truly at home. That was *her* fantasy world. And it was actually real.

But she loved George, and she respected his ambition. And while his deal-making was sometimes (usually) more for his own benefit than hers, she indulged him. Despite his penchant for showmanship, she reasoned that he always had her best interests at heart.

Abbie spent the next hour or more enduring the fawning of the gathered press. She graciously greeted all of the influential people that George had lined up. It reminded her very much of her debutant ball. And was just as excruciating.

Eventually, however, she was able to break away. George went off to smoke cigars and field offers with various agents and studio bigwigs. She was finally able to get a drink and mingle on her own.

"Congrats, Abbie," she heard a semi-familiar voice call out. "You got the man. The trophy. The whole nine yards."

Abbie turned around to find herself face-to-face with Leonore Lamonte, Society columnist for the *Daily Crusader*. With her dark hair pulled back into a tight bun and a skin-tight dress that she'd just purchased in Beverly Hills for the occasion, she fit right in with the Hollywood elite.

A distant relative of the blue-blooded Lamonte family, Leonore had parlayed her famous last name into a cushy job at the paper. She rather enjoyed her perch as the only gal reporter there. That is until a certain redhead had come along jockeying for a spot on the crime beat.

"Leonore, what a surprise," Abbie greeted her. On the one hand, it was nice to actually see a familiar face. And the only reporter who didn't want to talk about her "Hollywood career." On the downside, she immediately broached a topic that was even more uncomfortable.

"So, a little bird told me..." (this was usually shorthand for someone she'd paid off) "that a certain former suitor of yours came all the way out here to California to see you win the race."

Abbie just offered a pleasant smile and replied, "Isn't that what you did, as well?"

"I suppose you could say that," Leonore answered with feigned grace. "But I'm just a friend. So, any chance of a rendezvous? Perhaps even a reconciliation, dot dot dot?"

"No," Abbie told her politely and took the opportunity to move on. Familiar face or no. "Now, if you'll excuse me."

She walked off in no particular direction. Her eyes quickly searched the room for George, but he was nowhere to be seen. Then she remembered that he was already off wheeling and dealing.

She was sure that little episode would be top news in Leonore's society column the next morning. Of greater concern, however, was that Brent was there in Los Angeles.

She hadn't seen or heard from him since India. And, truth be told, she had no intention of ever seeing him again.

But since he was there, he would most certainly contact her.

Sure enough, when she returned alone to her suite to retire for the night, she found it. Among all the massive congratulatory bouquets she had received, there was a tiny arrangement of three white roses wrapped in paper. Just like he'd sent her many times before.

She shuddered to think what would be written on the card. She knew he wanted her back. But those days were in the past with no chance of return. She took a deep breath before she opened it.

"Let's meet up to-morrow. Catch up on old times. BRG."

VICKY parked behind the Terminal City Police Department and walked around to the front. It was a wide, three-story brick building that took up most of the block. The facade was at once both flat and ornamental. However, the first floor windows had arches built into the brickwork and the rest had distinctive stone work above.

The two ends of the building jutted out just far enough to allow for a single window on each floor. The effect was that of a large block on each end. The left side had two parking bays for automobiles. One for an ambulance and the other for a patrol car. In the event of any confusion, they were labeled in carved stone. At the opposite end was the entrance. It was a set of double doors framed by a pair of columns and a peaked portico overhead. Which was appropriately labeled "Police Department."

She'd been there only once before. Just a week prior, in fact. Digging for any tidbit she could find on the Man in Black. All of which had gotten her more good-natured kidding than results. This time, however, she had a lot of questions regarding the Nails McCarthy shooting. And she figured this was as good a place as any to start.

Her hunch was confirmed when she spotted Charlie Hecht and Ben Gelbart outside the main entrance. They were having a smoke with a couple of uniformed cops and getting an earful about who-knows-what. Then Charlie slipped a few bills into their pockets as they went back inside. *So, that's how you get your scoops*, Vicky thought.

"You're in the wrong place, Doll," Charlie smirked as she sauntered up. "This is a police station. Ain't no society types around here!"

His disdain didn't keep him from taking in the view. Or blocking her path as she tried to enter.

"So, where's Old Chester?" he asked, feigning puzzlement. "Ain't you supposed to be shadowing him? Having trouble keeping up?"

"Can it, Abercrombie," Vicky snapped back. "And get out of my way before I make you."

Charlie threw his hands up. "My pleasure, Doll Face. But listen, you up need someone to teach you the ropes, I'll be glad to show you *everything* I know. And then some."

"Oh yeah?" she asked. "Like how the *Standard* had to pull all its papers and run a separate edition this morning?"

That shut them up. Vicky shoved him aside and pushed her way in.

CHERRY NOSE CAIFANO took a long, savory puff on his cigar as he sat up in his hospital bed at the Our Lady of Mercy Infirmary. Vito Spats had brought him a new box and sat down in the chair next to him.

The Infirmary was a small hospital in the South Side dedicated to aiding the poor, sick, and injured. It was run by the nearby Catholic church and staffed primarily by nuns. Despite the desperate need for any available bed, Cherry Nose was able to secure a private room, where he'd spent the last several weeks.

"Hear they put a few in Nails McCarthy," Cherry Nose commented as he took another puff. "Can't say he didn't have it coming."

"Only three," Spats informed him.

"I took seven and I'm still here," Cherry Nose scoffed. "Gonna take more than that to take me down."

"You're looking better," Spats commented. "Think you might go home soon?"

"That's what the Doc says," Cherry Nose confirmed. "But I still gotta rest a while. Think I might head down to Florida. Doc says the sunshine'll do me good."

Vito Spats got up, checked the hallway, and shut the door. He'd left Fingers Scarrone down by the Nurse's station to make sure they remained undisturbed.

"You're up awful early, Spats," Cherry Nose observed. "Something tells me this ain't just a social call."

"Not exactly," Spats confirmed.

"Not that I'm complaining," Cherry Nose added. "After looking at these penguins all day, I gotta say, it's nice to see a friendly face."

"You hear Whitey managed to slip by again?" Spats asked.

"Who hasn't?" Cherry Nose asked with a grin, then held a pillow to his chest. It still hurt to laugh. Even a small chuckle.

"Got every copper in this city looking for him," Spats continued, "still nothing. Probably holed up in Chinatown somewhere."

"Good place to hide," Cherry Nose agreed. "So, you gonna rattle a few Chinamen? They don't talk easy, you know."

Spats stood up and paced uncomfortably. Just thinking about it roiled him up inside. "Jack wants us to keep our hands clean, especially after this whole Nails business."

Cherry Nose looked back at him with surprise. "That sure ain't the way we used to do things."

"Big Jack just keeps going on about that ace he's got."

"Oh, that old thing," Cherry Nose commented.

Spats sat back down and sighed in exasperation. "Back in the old days, when I was just starting to make my bones, if there was a problem, we handled it. No getting someone else to do the job. We got things done. And we got it done fast."

"You think Big Jack is slipping, don't you?" Cherry Nose asked.

CHAPTER SIX

VICKY wormed her way into the cramped foyer of the Southside Precinct. The interior was perfectly utilitarian. Beige walls, a staircase leading to the floors above, and a very large wooden reception desk. Standing behind it was Desk Sergeant Coffey. His graying hair and a paunchy middle hinted at just how long he'd been there.

"What can I do for you, Miss Rose?" he asked through a bushy moustache that hid most of his mouth. "Come to see about your mystery phantom again?"

"No," she replied through gritted teeth. "I want to talk to somebody. Got a few questions about the Nails McCarthy shooting."

Coffey immediately beamed with pride. "That Detective Flynn, he's lucky to be alive! They don't make 'em like him every day."

"Right," Vicky nodded, doing her best to play along. "Actually, I really just have one question. What kind of gun did Nails use to shoot Flynn?"

Coffey thought for a moment. But it was soon clear that he didn't have an answer. "Well, I don't exactly know. You'd have to ask Detective Flynn himself."

"And he's not here, is he?" she asked, already knowing the answer full well.

"No, Miss," Coffey answered. "Detective Flynn is still recovering. Won't be back for a few days yet."

Strike one.

"How about the other officer that was there?" Vicky

asked, never one to give up. "Shayne? Can I talk to him?"

Sergeant Coffey checked his records. "Officer Shayne's not in yet. Nope. Haven't seen him."

Strike two.

"Okay then," Vicky posited in one final attempt. "Didn't you collect the gun into evidence? Don't you have any kind of records you could check?"

"I just work the desk here, Miss Rose," he affirmed. "Like I said, you'll have to talk to Detective Flynn."

Strike three.

"I intend to," she retorted.

OFFICER SHAYNE nursed a cup of coffee as he stood at his kitchen counter. He took a sip and reacted in disgust before pouring it out. It had long gone cold as he'd stared out the window. He could have used something stronger anyway.

There was a car parked across the street that he didn't recognize. Two men inside. They'd been there all morning. Didn't need to be a policeman to know that something wasn't right.

"Everything okay, Poppa?" his wife, Agnes, surprised him. "You should have left twenty minutes ago."

Agnes Shayne was a fine woman and a good wife. After his years in the Marines, it had taken him some time to settle down. They'd met in the neighborhood where she worked as a domestic and he'd walked the beat. They got better acquainted in church, which relieved many in the congregation. Like her husband (though still a good ten years younger), she'd been in no rush for matrimony. She was pious woman who kept a good house.

"Yes, of course. I'm fine," he reassured her. "Just a little tired is all."

"Maybe you shouldn't have stayed out so late," she commented with a wry smile. She knew he had come home with alcohol on his breath. But she also knew that it was such a rare occasion, he'd probably had a good reason for it.

The silence was broken when their ten-year-old son, Bobby Junior, galloped into the kitchen with his toy six-shooters blazing. He wore his red cowboy hat and had his shiny Sheriff's badge pinned to his shirt.

"Hey, Pa!" Bobby asked excitedly. "You going to shoot any more gangsters to-day? Think one day you'll be a G-Man?"

Agnes bristled at her son's enthusiasm. Shayne just shook his head. This wasn't the way he wanted to be a hero to his boy.

Shayne put a hand on Bobby's shoulder and knelt down to quell his enthusiasm. "Listen son, I didn't shoot anybody. That was my boss, Detective Flynn."

Shayne paused for a moment and searched for the right words. He looked Bobby in the eye, but the words still weren't there. All these past ten years he'd tried to teach his son about honesty, integrity, and doing what was right.

Shayne loved being Bobby's hero. But on this particular day, he didn't much feel like one.

"Detective Flynn only fired his weapon because he felt our lives were in danger," he explained. "That's something we never want to do unless we absolutely have to. Understand?"

If only that were true, Shayne thought. He'd never before knowingly lied to his son. And it made him sick in the pit of his stomach to have just done it then.

Bobby Junior fired his pistols and ran off. Shayne stood up and looked out the window again. The car was still there.

Maybe it was more than the lying that made him feel sick.

Agnes could tell immediately. "You don't look well, Poppa. Maybe you should stay home."

She quickly touched his cheek with the back of her hand. How he loved the softness of her skin.

"No, that would be worse," he told her.

VICKY had waited in the Precinct entry hall for a good while before her patience finally got the best of her. She'd been keeping an eye out for Officer Shayne, but there'd been no sign of him.

She'd noticed that Hecht and Gelbart were still snooping around. Clearly they had an "in" with the cops and knew something she didn't. Otherwise, they would have already flown the coop.

Vicky charged back up to Desk Sergeant Coffey. "What time does this Shayne get in, anyway?" she asked in frustration. "Has he called in sick?"

"No, Miss," Coffey answered, just as frustrated, but for the opposite reason. "I'm afraid I don't know."

Vicky had barely made it back to the bench before Hecht and Gelbart suddenly reappeared from down the hall.

Next up was a small parade of semi-familiar faces from the North Side. Dapper Sheridan, Mossy Egan, Spike Kinney, and Cockeye Dunne. Limping in at the rear was Kid Yellow Newman. They were escorted by a handful of uniforms. Two of which Vicky recognized immediately. They were the cops Charlie had paid off earlier.

She wasn't about to let it get to her. The luck of the Irish had just swung in her favor.

As the young hoods collected their things and prepared to leave police custody, Vicky was surprised to learn that all four had posted a grand each in bail money.

"Say, Squint," Hecht inquired. "What'dya say you give me the whole scoop of what happened last night? You know, tell me your side of the story?"

Squint Mulligan grabbed his things and brushed past Charlie. "Forget it, Bub! I ain't seen nuthin'!"

Gelbart didn't fare any better. "Mind telling me who posted your bail?"

Spike Kinney barked in response, "Nuthin' doin'! I ain't talked to the coppers, and I sure as hell ain't about to spill to some short stack newshound!"

Vicky managed to snag Dapper before he made it out the door. Luckily, she had one weapon in her arsenal that the boys most certainly didn't. Feminine charm. It also didn't hurt that, with her auburn hair, her own Irish heritage showed through.

And she didn't even have to worry about Hecht and Gelbart overhearing. They were so deep in the accepted narrative they were willfully blinded to any other theories on the truth.

"Pardon me, Dapper," she asked coquettishly. "I was wondering if I could ask you a few questions."

"Sure thing, Doll," Dapper replied, tipping his bowler to one side and giving her the once over. "You can ask me anything you like."

Vicky got straight to the point. "Was Nails even packing in his office?"

Dapper was taken aback. "Now, why would you ask me something like that?"

She really poured on the charm. Whatever it took to get a scoop. "Come on, you can tell me. Won't you help a girl out? Please?"

"Far be it from me to ignore a beautiful dame," Dapper replied with a wolfish grin.

But before he could get another word out, Hecht rushed over and interrupted. "Say, Dapper! Don't let this one snake charm you. She's a reporter!"

If they were going to come up empty-handed, he wasn't about to let a skirt steal her own scoop right from under their noses. No matter how wacky it was.

Dapper took a step back and looked her over again. "You don't say? When did the *Standard* start hiring dames to chase the news?"

"The *Crusader*, actually," Vicky corrected. "So, was he packing or not?"

"Nice try, but I ain't telling you, Sweetheart," Dapper pushed her aside. Then he turned back to Hecht on his way out the door. "Thanks, Pal."

Vicky just glowered at Hecht. "You bastard, Charlie."

OFFICER SHAYNE quickly steered his patrol car into an alley and screeched to a halt. He slammed on the brakes so fast that the black car following almost ran into him.

Shayne jumped out, unsnapped his holster, and gripped his night stick as he rushed the other vehicle.

Willie Potatoes quickly stepped out and stood behind the open door. Only one hand was visible. The one in the sling. "There a problem officer?" Willie asked.

"You don't have to follow me. Or watch my house," Shayne barked. "I get the message."

Willie just grinned back. "What message?"

"Don't play stupid with me, Willie. I know who you are.

And I know what this is all about. You tell Big Jack he doesn't have to worry. I know how the system works around here. You can lean on me all you want. Just stay the hell away from my family, you got it?"

Willie threw up his hands, innocent as a lamb, and moved where Shayne could see him. "I'm afraid you got me all wrong, Officer."

He had something in his right hand. But it most definitely wasn't a gun.

"Big Jack just wanted me to congratulate you on a fine bit of police work," Willie continued as he moved closer. "He appreciates everything you do to keep this city safe. He'd like to keep it that way."

Willie got all the way up to Shayne and stuffed a roll of bills into the pocket of the lawman's coat. Right below his badge.

"Why don't you go out and buy your wife something nice?" Willie asked with all the charm of a used car salesman. "I'm sure she'd appreciate it."

Shayne just stood there and glowered back. His first instinct was to throw the money right back at the henchman. It was a good instinct.

His job finished, Willie sauntered back to his car. "By the way, we're opening a new place in just a few weeks. Called the Four Diamonds. You're welcome there any time. Drinks are on us."

Willie flashed one more oily, toothy grin before getting back in his car. "You should bring that lovely wife of yours to the grand opening. We'll make sure you get a special invitation. Have a swell day now, Officer."

VICKY buried her frustration, downed another couple of pills, and went back to her desk. Frank was fond of saying, "If I see your face in the office, then you're not doing your job." And since it was already past lunchtime, Vicky felt she had taken that credo to heart.

The city room was filled with suspicious looks and whispers just as soon as she walked in. It didn't take a clairvoyant to know who was the main topic. Especially Lyons, who sat at her desk.

"Where the heck have you been, Doll?" he asked. It didn't take a genius to see his "two martini lunch" had been just that and more.

"Doing your job," she said and tossed him the morning edition. Only when he picked it up, it wasn't the *Crusader*. Rather, it was the *Standard*, with a headline that screamed "NAILS McCARTHY KILLED IN POLICE SHOOTOUT."

Every other paper in town had scrambled all morning to put out an updated edition. Even so, that didn't make him feel any better about being bumped off the front page. Especially by a skirt who was still wet behind the ears.

Lyons got up and lit up a cigarette. "I'm gonna hit the streets. You know where to find me."

"Don't wait up," she retorted.

She was just about to head into Frank's office when Perry Phillips stopped her.

"Vick, you got a few messages," he informed her as he handed over a small stack of call slips. "Some character named Spider."

She let out a deep sigh of exasperation. "Yeah, keeps calling. Claims he's got information to sell. Thanks, Perry."

Vicky stuck the messages in her desk drawer and hustled into Frank's office. "Like this morning's headline?" she asked cheerily and plopped down into a chair.

"Lot better than the *Standard*'s, that's for sure," he praised. "Good work. Get anything downtown?"

"Not much," she grumbled. "Nails' crew is out on bail. Almost got Dapper to spill, till Charlie ratted me out."

"Talk to anybody with a badge?" Frank asked.

"Empty there, too," Vicky confessed. "Flynn's still out and Shayne never showed. I'm going to head down to the morgue and see what I can dig up."

"You hear the latest? Word is the Mayor wants to give those two a medal. Have a big ceremony down in Harrison Park."

Vicky shook her head in disbelief as she stood up. "Well, if that ain't a load of bushwa…"

"Listen Red," Frank stopped her before she could bolt. "I didn't pair you up with Lyons just for the fun of it. I know he's a handful, but he can still teach you plenty."

"So, you want me to get toasted in O'Doule's this afternoon?" she smirked.

"What I'm saying is," Frank countered, "you don't actually know *everything*. Lyons has been around the block and then some. You haven't even spent five minutes with the guy."

Vicky let out a huff of exasperation and replied, "Well, when he shows me an ounce of respect, I'll think about returning the favor."

"Don't hold your breath. And try not to spend too much time down in the basement," Frank ribbed.

CHAPTER SEVEN

ABBIE WENTWORTH greeted Worthington with a warm hug as she entered Brent's private bungalow at the Ambassador Hotel. Despite all that had passed between her and Brent, she still considered Worthington family.

The accommodations were very similar to her own suite, just larger and more private. The furnishings were sleek and modern, just what one would expect from the premiere hotel in Hollywood. The sliding glass doors in the living room led to a spacious, covered patio. It was surrounded by a high fence and decorated with potted palms.

She had a fair degree of dread regarding their reunion. She still hadn't forgiven him for his behavior in India. But with George off holding meetings at MGM, it seemed as good a time as any to get it over with.

And with Leonore flittering about the grounds on high alert for any little scoop that might cross her path, she also had to be extra cautious. Thankfully, the hotel staff was able to spirit her there via the private, underground hallway. It had been built for just such a purpose. And for when alcohol was illegal, of course.

She smiled at the older man anxiously. "So good to see you again, Worthington."

Worthington looked at her proudly, much like a father who'd seen his little girl grow up. "Likewise, Miss Abigail. You've grown more lovely than ever. And congratulations on a well-deserved win. Most impressive."

"Thank you, she said anxiously as her eyes darted about

the bungalow.

Of course, Brent was not immediately visible. Always the stickler for formality.

"I have to say," she stated, "this was an unexpected surprise. What brings you to Los Angeles?"

"I'm sure that's not difficult to surmise, Miss Abigail," he replied with an anxious smile. "Master Gregor is waiting on the patio, so permit me not to intrude. He has some... important news that he wishes to share. Though I do suggest that you may wish to sit down first."

Abbie gave him a puzzled look as he lead her through the bungalow. There was no telling what Brent had in store in his expected efforts to win her back. Part of her wished that she had never come, but there were things that needed to be said. The sooner the better.

"Miss Wentworth to see you, Sir," Worthington announced as they reached the glass doors of the covered patio.

"Good day, Miss Abigail," he nodded as he dismissed himself and closed the doors.

Brent was seated on the couch, his wheelchair off to the side. He wore a light suit and looked as handsome as she had ever seen him.

"Hello, Abbie," he said cordially. It was as if India had never happened. "Good to see you again."

"Hello Brent," she replied, more polite than warm. Just seeing him again brought back a flood of bad memories. She stood there for a long moment in awkward silence.

When she got mad, he well knew, she reverted to her upper crust upbringing and became terribly formal.

"Please, sit down," he offered.

"No thank you," she stated defiantly. "I can't stay long. I've a rather busy day, I'm afraid. George is expecting me for lunch."

"Can I get you anything?"

"No, I'm quite fine, thank you," she replied.

"You've cut your hair," he observed. He'd always liked it long, and had never imagined it otherwise. It was disconcerting to see her that way. Like she was a completely different woman.

She, in turn, noticed the ornate red-stone ring on his

right hand. She was tempted to point it out. But didn't want to do anything to prolong the conversation.

"If you don't mind, I really don't have much time," she stated. "What was it you wanted to see me about?"

"Yes, of course," he said, shifting in his seat. "Two things, actually. First of all, I wanted to apologize — "

"I received your letters," she interrupted.

"Apologize in person," he continued. "There was no excuse for my behavior. I'm just very, very sorry for everything I said. And did."

"Yes, so was I," she quickly shot back with no offer of acceptance. "And the second?"

"Something I need you to see," he replied.

He gathered himself for a moment. She could have sworn the ring on his hand actually glowed. Or maybe it was just a reflection from the sunlight above. She definitely felt the slight chill in the air.

Brent pushed himself to the edge of the couch. She instinctively moved to get his chair.

He quickly put up a hand to stop her. "Thank you, but there's no need."

She watched in wide-eyed wonder as he clutched the edge of the couch. Then he slowly, shakily, struggled to his feet.

Until at last he was actually standing.

Her knees quickly gave out. Then she was the one who dropped to the floor.

All she could do was stare up at him in wide-eyed wonder.

He walked carefully over. Then offered a hand to help her up.

Her instinct was not to take it. Not because of her anger towards him. But because she didn't immediately believe what she was actually seeing.

Instead, she quickly stood up on her own and backed away. She struggled to speak, but the words completely escaped her.

"H-how?" was all she could stammer.

"It's a long story," he told her. "But suffice it to say, I found a treatment, if you will, that actually, finally provided results."

DENNY's eyes lit up just as soon as Vicky set foot in his office. She found it a tad embarrassing and had already received no end of teasing. Not just from Frank, but most especially from Leonore. She'd asked him more than once to just play it cool, but it just wasn't in his nature.

"What can you tell me about Detective Sergeant Flynn?" Vicky asked, doing her best to keep the conversation all business.

"Knew you'd be coming," he gushed as he handed her a folder stuffed full of clippings. "Already pulled it for you. Long, decorated career. Mostly just praise. At least as far as the paper's concerned."

"Well, that doesn't help me much," Vicky groused as she flipped through the contents. "No reprimands? Suspensions? Links to the Mob?"

"Nothing that I saw," Denny confirmed. "A little too polished if you ask me. Like he paid someone at the paper to just write a bunch of puff pieces."

"My thoughts exactly," Vicky proclaimed as she shut the folder and handed it back to him. "How about this Shayne? Anything on him?"

"Oh, he's a bonafide hero," Denny explained as he handed her another folder, this one much thinner.

"Oh?" Vicky asked as she took the file and quickly perused the handful of clippings inside.

"Lied about his age and signed up for the War. Drove an ambulance in France," Denny provided. "Only that's not the heroic part."

Vicky dug through the few articles. They were all from a few years earlier, well before she had moved to Terminal City. The most recent detailed his heroic status.

A young mother was at home late one night with her three small children. Her ex-husband, who'd been out of work for the better part of a year, showed up dead drunk and broke down the door. For some reason, he was convinced she had another man in the house. He threatened her with a gun, beat her with his fists, and tore up the whole house. The kids all hid in a bedroom closet.

She locked herself in the room with the children. She had just managed to call the police when he broke down that door, too, and shot her. That's when the line went dead.

Fortunately, several of the neighbors had already telephoned as well. Shayne and his partner at the time, a young rookie who'd been on the force less than a year, arrived just a few minutes afterwards.

The ex-husband shouted for them to stay out of it and took a few shots at them, too. Shayne's partner froze up and hid behind the car. But Shayne wasn't about to leave the kids inside the house.

He'd just readied his pistol when they heard the mother scream inside. That's when he threw caution to the wind and rushed the front door.

According to the articles, Shayne took a bullet in the shoulder shortly after getting inside. But he still managed to pummel the ex-husband and subdue him in short order.

Another squad car showed up minutes later. Right when Shayne came out with the mother and all three children. She'd been shot in the leg and badly beaten, but was, thankfully, still alive.

She told the waiting reporters that her husband had pulled the children from the closet and threatened to kill them in front of her. But thanks to Shayne's quick action, all three were unharmed.

Vicky just shook her head in disbelief. "So wait a minute, this guy rescues three kids, takes a bullet, and he just gets a pat on the back. And *now* he gets a medal?"

ABBIE struggled to regain her footing. Brent reached out to help her, but was still on uneasy ground himself. She backed away and steadied herself on the couch.

"You did it!" she blurted out with astonishment.

She walked around him, looked for some explanation. Mirrors, wires, anything. Her mind was still unable to comprehend it. It was like magic. But it was actually real.

"After all these years. You finally did it." She looked back at his wheelchair. "Is it… permanent?"

"Somewhat," he answered cryptically.

As if on cue, his legs quivered. She instinctively reached out and helped him back to the couch. He looked at her with eyes that offered so much more than deep appreciation.

"Thank you."

She had to reach for the chair and sit down herself. Again the words failed her. She was so stunned.

Worthington had been right.

"I'm just so happy for you..." she stammered. "I'm still in just total disbelief, I don't know what to say."

The ring glowed brighter, and he pushed himself up again. This time stronger, more assured of his footing. This time she was sure that the glow wasn't a reflection. She felt a deeper chill.

God only knew what kind of witchcraft he'd gotten himself into. She instinctively took another step back, wondering if she should be afraid.

"This is all for you," he said proudly.

No matter the miracle she'd just witnessed, Abbie stood angry and defiant. She wasn't about to suddenly forgive and forget. Not after the pain she'd experienced.

"No, it isn't," she stood firm. "It never was."

This was not the reaction he had expected.

"I told you that. Over and over," she reacted. "I didn't *care* that you couldn't walk. I *never* did. But you did. And you let it become the most important thing in your life. More important than me."

He just stood there in stunned silence. She stepped towards the patio doors, ready to leave. Ready to escape once and for all.

"I wish we could make up for what happened," she confessed. "But it's too late. I've moved on in my life."

"It's not too late," he countered. "I'm sorry for what I did. I'm sorry for all of it. I'll apologize every day for the rest of my life if I have to. But don't you see? This is behind us now. We can move on together."

"I married George," she stated emphatically.

Now it was Brent's turn to stare back in stunned silence.

"Last week, actually," she said nervously. "We wanted to keep it quiet. Until after the race. I thought you should know before you read it in the papers. I'm sorry."

Brent said nothing.

He just closed his eyes and clenched his fists. Abbie knew that look well. She'd seen it time and again. It was the look of a man utterly defeated by his circumstances. Powerless to fight back in any way.

The air grew suddenly cold. The plants, furniture, and overhang began to rumble.

She quickly reached for the door. Frantically looked about as the ceiling shook overhead.

"Master Gregor!" Worthington called out. He reached for Abbie and took her hand.

Brent opened his eyes. The tremors stopped.

"Are you all right, Miss Abigail?" Worthington asked.

"Oh, my goodness!" she exclaimed nervously. "Did you feel that? My first quake!"

She noticed that Worthington hadn't inquired about Brent's safety.

"Yes," Worthington responded, glowering at Brent. "Thank heavens it was but a small one."

"Well, it was good to see you again, Brent," she said bravely. "I just can't believe this miracle. I hope it finally brings you the happiness for which you've been searching."

"I'll show you out, Miss Abigail," Worthington offered.

She stood there quietly for a moment, not sure what else to say. Then she turned and left.

But before Worthington could follow behind her, Brent instructed, "I want to take the train back home. Immediately."

CHAPTER EIGHT

EARLY the next morning, Vicky shoved her way through the throng of press and onlookers crammed into the lobby of the Clark County Courthouse. Like all municipal buildings in Terminal City, it was a multi-story, neoclassical structure with white granite columns. The inside was a combination of white marble flooring and walls with dark wooden doors. It's desired effect was to impress and impose, which it did with equal measure.

"Lady coming through!" Some men actually stepped aside, or attempted to, at least. Others, she just had to bulldoze her way past.

She managed to bump into Ben Gelbart extra hard as she worked her way to the front. It was less effective than a lit cigarette, but effective nonetheless.

"Hey, watch it!" Gelbart squealed. "Get here early next time, will ya?"

"Hey, Doll Face," Charlie retorted, "you can bump into me any time."

Every reporter in Terminal City was there, except for Chester Lyons. He was out nursing his usual morning hangover. But as Vicky found out later, he'd already got most of the story the night before from his contacts at O'Doule's. And the byline, to boot.

She landed right next to her old compatriots from the press room, Morty Cohen and Bill Higgs. A welcome chance for them to get out of the basement and cover some real news for a change.

"What's this all about? Any idea?" Vicky asked.

"Word from upstairs is they're going to charge Nails McCarthy," Morty explained.

Higgs just shrugged. "Have to make it look good before the big awards ceremony."

Vicky and Morty nodded in surprised agreement. Pretty suspicious indeed.

The room erupted into a barrage of shouted questions as District Attorney Everett "Doc" Milford, several of his Assistant DA's, and Chief LaSalle made their way to the podium. Officer Shayne was noticeably absent. Noticeable to Vicky, at least.

Doc Milford was immediately pummeled with a flurry of questions. He raised a hand and called out, "Gentlemen, gentlemen," until everyone finally quieted down.

Morty commented, "They forget there's a lady present."

"It's not unintentional, believe me," Vicky informed him.

"It is my duty as District Attorney to inform you gentlemen of the press that as of one hour ago, James McCarthy, alias "Nails" McCarthy, has been placed under arrest."

"What's the charge?" Charlie shouted.

Doc Milford continued, undeterred, bathed in the continual glow of flash bulbs. "The charges are as follows. Two counts of resisting arrest. Two counts of assaulting an officer of the law. And two counts of attempted murder."

The crowd again erupted into a barrage of questions. *"Is Nails going to pull through? Any luck finding Whitey O'Leary? How's Detective Flynn? If Nails lives, will you take this case to trial? Will you go for the death penalty?"*

This time, Vicky was content to just sit back and watch. Particularly since the loudness of the room did nothing for her growing headache.

She knew it was all for show. Had to wonder if most of those other newshounds (Morty and Higgs excepted) were really gullible enough to gladly accept whatever lie they were told. With Hecht and Gelbart, she already knew the answer.

All of which only made the pain in her head even worse.

"You okay?" Morty asked. Leave it to him to notice.

"Yeah, don't worry about me," she told him. "Just a little headache is all."

Of course, he was smart enough to know better.

ELYSE THOMPKINS worked diligently to put fresh sheets on the bed and tidy up the master bedroom in the Gregor Mansion. Mr. Worthington had sent a telegram that morning that Master Gregor's trip had been cut short and to have the house ready for his return, post-haste.

A dark haired, sensible girl, she had no family of her own. She'd worked for Master Gregor since she was fourteen, just before he left for college and long after the tragedy. Of the housekeepers, next to Mrs. Poole, she'd been there the longest.

It was quite the privilege to clean the Master's room, especially while he was out. It showed a level of trust not afforded to the other maids. Currently, only she and Mrs. Poole had been granted that privilege. And with Mrs. Poole's failing health, she was the likely successor to her position.

She was nearly finished when Mollie Callaghan breezed in for a look. "Readying the master's bedroom, eh?" Mollie teased, with more than a hint of mischief in her voice. She knew of Elyse's affinity for Master Gregor and liked to tease her at every opportunity.

Mollie was younger, with strawberry blonde hair and a sense of adventure that would likely one day get her into trouble. She somehow managed to look quite fetching even in her staid, black maid's uniform. Her mother worked for the Kennellys and her younger sister would do the same once she completed the eighth grade.

"Come now," Elyse reprimanded. "You know you're not supposed to be in here. If Mrs. Poole caught you, we'd both be out on our ears."

"Don't you worry none," Mollie shrugged. "If I hear the elevator, I'll beat it. Just wanted to have a little peak is all."

Mollie ran her hands along the crisp bed sheet as Elyse worked to tuck the corners.

"Mighty big bed for just one man," Mollie commented.

"Think he ever gets tired of sleeping in here alone?"

"I wouldn't know," Elyse retorted. "But as long as you're in here, you can give me a hand."

Instead, Mollie impulsively threw herself on the huge bed. She stretched out in every direction to better appreciate its size and comfort.

"Now look what you've done!" Elyse panicked. "Get off of there!"

"Don't get your nickers in an uproar," Mollie chided. "Don't think you haven't dreamed about it yourself."

"Hurry up, before Bridget sees you!"

Mollie patted the mattress with a mischievous grin. Elyse just stood firm and impatiently waited until Mollie finally got up.

Elyse hurriedly straightened the sheets and threw the blanket across. Mollie grabbed a corner and helped her finish making it.

"So, why do you think Master Gregor's coming back from Hollywood, eh?" Mollie asked. "Hadn't been there hardly more than a day."

"We don't even know that he went to Hollywood," Elyse replied.

"Of course, he did," Mollie asserted. "With the flying race and all, where else would he have gone? Think Miss Wentworth turned him down?"

"I wouldn't know," Elyse commented. "It's none of my business. And it's none of yours, either."

"Well," Mollie stated, "you can bet he'll be in a right fowl mood when he gets back."

"All the more reason for you to not be in here," Elyse added as they finished the blanket and went to work stuffing the many pillows into their cases.

"Can't say as I'd mind stepping in," Mollie commented. "He's right handsome, even for a cripple. And being rich as Midas certainly helps. I could get over that chair, easy."

Elyse could only roll her eyes. "Pray the good Lord doesn't hear what comes out of that mouth of yours."

As if on cue, Bridget poked her head in the door. "He's looking stronger these days," she observed happily.

Elyse threw her hands up in frustration.

At barely sixteen, Bridget Moreau was the youngest and most recent addition to the staff. A fair-haired, doe-eyed girl of French Canadian stock, she was very much a young girl on the verge of womanhood.

"Notice that nurse of his doesn't come around anymore," Bridget observed.

"He's strong enough, I'd say," Mollie added with a wicked smile.

Elyse didn't have to ask her meaning. "Forget it, Mollie. A man of Mr. Gregor's standing would only be interested in a single night from the likes of you. Nothing more."

Having had quite enough, she hustled them towards the door. "Now out, both of you!"

"Oh, I don't know," Mollie quipped. "I'd make sure he come back for more."

NOT TO BE outdone by the DA's office, Chief of Police Harry LaSalle hosted a press briefing of his own later that afternoon in the main lobby of Terminal City General. The grand occasion was the release of Detective Sergeant Michael Flynn from hospital care. The up-side for LaSalle was that he got to be on stage for both events.

"Somebody's gonna get dizzy from all the grandstanding," Vicky quipped.

Attendance-wise, it was pretty much a repeat of the morning briefing with all of the usual suspects. Charlie, Gelbart, Morty, Higgs, and every other reporter in town.

Chester Lyons even managed to make an appearance, clearly feeling no pain. "Look who finally showed up," he grumbled.

"Made it here sober, too," she retorted. Then stood with her old compatriots from the *Standard*. Even the prickly Higgs was more welcoming.

Most surprising was the appearance of Officer Shayne. He just stood silently in the back, looking ever more like an Easter Island statue.

The crowd of reporters erupted in a burst of cheers for the appearance of Detective Sergeant Flynn. He was escorted in a wheelchair (hospital protocol, nothing more) by two pretty, young nurses and Dr. Carol Nelson, the surgeon who'd patched-up him up.

"A woman doctor, what'dya know?" commented Higgs.

Vicky offered a biting retort, but was drowned out by the cacophony of celebration as they all clapped and shouted their congratulations. After many repeated calls for silence from Chief LaSalle, the crowd finally calmed down enough for Flynn to make his statement.

"I want to thank the wonderful Dr. Nelson here for her impressive skill and dedication to the medical field." Then he added with a schoolboy smile, "And I especially want to thank all of the lovely nurses that took such good care of me."

"You'd think he was shot three times," Higgs whispered. Vicky had to stifle a laugh. That made up for the slight a moment earlier.

Afterwards, LaSalle introduced Dr. Nelson, whom by this point was known by everyone in the city as "the woman doctor who'd saved Detective Flynn's life."

"Thank you, Detective Flynn, Chief LaSalle," she blushed. "I'd only like to say that I was just doing my job. And to, please, if you wouldn't mind, just take a break from the dangerous stuff for a while."

"Spoken like a true physician!" Flynn laughed. The gathered press brayed right along with him.

Vicky couldn't help but notice that Officer Shayne looked increasingly uncomfortable. But he put on a brave face, nonetheless. And did his best to at least look like he enjoyed the moment. But she knew a fake smile when she saw one.

At that point, LaSalle opened the field and the newshounds lobbied their questions. Each and every one of the softball variety.

"Detective Flynn, what's it like to be such a great hero? Detective Flynn, you gonna pitch for the Boilermen anytime soon? Detective Flynn, you ready for the shooting gallery at the State Fair?"

"What a bunch of barking seals," Vicky remarked. "Will nobody ask a decent question?"

"Most of these fellows only work for fish," Morty agreed.

She'd already gotten on LaSalle's bad side after the Nibley murder. But that wasn't about to stop her from wading in again.

"Detective Flynn," Vicky called out sweetly, "may I ask, what kind of gun did Nails have?"

Flynn was immediately taken aback. "What was that?"

Vicky got more pointed: "What kind of gun did Nails have? I keep asking, but no one can tell me. Surely an officer of your experience would know something like that."

LaSalle jumped right into the fray. "Listen, Sweetheart, if you're implying that — "

Morty went to interject, but Vicky stopped him. "I'm not implying anything," she retorted. "I just asked a simple question. What kind of gun was it?"

"The kind that shot me in the arm!" Flynn snapped back. "What kind do you think?" The other reporters burst into laughter.

Not a one of them even cares about the truth, Vicky thought. They just tow the line, do as they're told. No wonder this city is so corrupt.

Gelbart asked, "What're you trying to do, Doll? Ruin everything? This man's a hero!"

Judging by the round of applause that followed, he clearly echoed the sentiments of the room.

"Say Lyons," Charlie retorted, "might want to keep your little gal in check."

Lyons just shrugged them off. He was more than content to let Vicky fall flat on her face.

She felt her headache return.

BRENT GREGOR stared out of the dining room window of his private rail car. His uneaten breakfast waited on the nearby table, already cold. The glass of scotch, however, was empty. There was only one thought on his mind.

Abbie.

He'd imagined his return trip home so much differently.

After all he'd been through the last few years, and especially after the miracle that she'd just witnessed, he never once considered that she would reject him.

Never.

And yet, despite all that had just transpired the day before, he still couldn't yet bring himself to face the obvious.

That there was no winning her back.

So many questions swirled through his mind. Questions for which he had no answers. Had he really and truly lost her forever? Had it been in India, as he had for so long believed? Or had he been mistaken all that time? Had it actually been three years earlier? That night at Vicedomini's?

Had all of his efforts and the thousands of dollars spent trying to walk again been a complete waste? The clinic in Austria? The faith healer in Los Angeles? The shaman in India? And even the gypsy woman in Terminal City?

And if that were the case, who was truly to blame?

He didn't want to believe it.

He simply couldn't believe it.

He took a last swallow and watched the arid, barren landscape of the Southwest outside. With every passing mile, he felt her move further and further away from him.

Worthington sat on the far side of the car and watched with concern. Even in the smaller quarters of the rail car, he still practiced decorum and took his meals after Master Gregor. Which was made all the more difficult by Brent's apparent lack of appetite.

"I'm so terribly sorry, Sir," Worthington consoled. "I can only imagine how difficult this is for you."

Brent didn't answer. His attention still fixed out the window.

"I do wish you would eat something," Worthington implored. "You still need your strength. And drink less, perhaps."

"Thank you, Worthington," Brent finally replied. "But I'm just not at all hungry."

Worthington got up, took Brent's plate, and delivered it to the adjoining kitchen. "Would you be more comfortable in the lounge, Sir?"

He waited a long moment before Brent offered a tearful response. "I just don't understand, Worthington. I was sure that when she saw me walk, that everything would be different."

Worthington stumbled on just how to respond. As a bachelor of many years, he was ill prepared for matters of the heart. "Forgive my saying so, Sir. But perhaps your physical handicap was never the issue."

That's what Abbie had tried to tell him many times over. And he had resolutely refused to listen.

The last thing Brent was prepared to face was the truth.

DR. NELSON walked back into the blessedly empty hospital lobby. Following the press briefing, the young nurses had wheeled Detective Flynn out of the front door to a waiting police car. He was given a full escort home with lights and sirens. The other reporters had followed right behind and bathed the entire event in a sea of flashbulbs.

As much as she had enjoyed the press attention and adulation, it was time to get back to the business of being a surgeon. There were other patients who needed her attention. With problems greater than a superficial bullet wound. Patients that wouldn't involve a throng of reporters to capture her every word.

She'd just turned down the hallway back to her office when she heard a friendly, female voice call out to her. "Doctor Nelson?"

"Yes?" she replied, happy to respond. Then just as quickly, her expression changed. "Oh, it's you."

Vicky stopped her before she could walk away. She'd already made a terrible first impression at the press conference. She couldn't imagine that this encounter would be any better. "Please, Doctor," Vicky implored. "I just want to ask you a few questions."

Dr. Nelson let out a sigh of exasperation and thought for a long moment. She knew how tough it was to be a woman doctor. Couldn't be easy as a woman reporter, either, she reasoned. "Make it fast," she instructed and shook her head.

"Would you happen to still have the bullet from Detective Flynn?" Vicky asked.

"Oh, no," she replied. "There was no bullet. It barely touched him."

"I see," Vicky replied. Not exactly the answer she'd expected. She gently rubbed her temple.

Dr. Nelson nodded and turned to leave. "Now, I really

must be going."

"Just one other question, please," Vicky stopped her. She hesitated a moment, afraid to even ask. Then she whispered, "Is it possible that the wound was self-inflicted?"

Dr. Nelson's eyes grew big as saucers. She quickly pulled Vicky aside. "Miss Rose! I wouldn't even begin to suggest —"

"I'm not trying to suggest anything," Vicky retorted. "I just want to know, and this is completely off the record. I promise you. Is it possible?"

"You swear this is off the record?" Dr. Nelson asked.

"Yes, absolutely," Vicky reassured her.

The respected surgeon paused for another long moment. She stared at the floor and collected her thoughts. "I have no reason whatsoever to doubt Detective Flynn's account of the events. However..."

Vicky listened with heightened anticipation. She wasn't sure she even wanted to hear the answer. But she knew she had to.

"Yes," Doctor Nelson confirmed, "it is *remotely* possible."

"Thank you," Vicky replied with gushing gratitude.

"And if I see one word of that in your paper, you'll hear from my lawyer," Nelson added. "Now if you'll excuse me, I must get back to my patients."

"You won't," Vicky promised her.

"And you really should see a doctor about that headache," Dr. Nelson added as she walked away. "*Another* doctor."

CHAPTER NINE

Five Years Prior.

THE SUMMER following Abbie's confession about flying, she and Brent both returned to Terminal City and near empty houses of their childhoods. Abbie's parents had moved to Europe. Her older brother, Billy, had begun working for his uncle at the bank and taken his own apartment downtown.

Worthington had gotten used to not having Brent around. The older valet spent most of his time doing charity work at the Chinatown Parish. Nanny Miriam had already moved on (she'd have been so excited to see them together) and some of the staff had been let go. Away from school and chaperones of any kind, the two teenagers were largely unsupervised.

Despite this, Brent felt the responsibility of maintaining his visits to his mother. He'd been informed that she'd worsened while he was away, but wasn't sure what to expect.

Worthington had planned to cancel his weekly Parish visit and escort Brent there, but was rather surprised when Abbie volunteered to do so in his stead. That was when he realized the true nature of their relationship. He had to wonder what the future held for this blossoming romance.

Only time would tell.

On their prior visits, Worthington spoke privately with Dr. Kobler, Mrs. Gregor's attending psychiatrist. While

Brent waited uncomfortably by himself in the cold, sterile lobby. The Desk Nurse never said a word or offered to make his wait more palatable. Even worse were the occasional screams from down the hall.

It was equally uncomfortable for Abbie. She remarked how horrid it was that his mother was locked up in such an awful place. Furthermore, she pitied Brent for having to go there all those years. She recounted all those times Julius Kennelly had teased him. And confessed that this was when she first saw Brent as something more than that terrible little boy with whom she'd been forced to play.

She actually had second thoughts about even staying there. Her instinct had been to leave and just wait in the car. But she didn't want to leave Brent to face this filial duty on his own. And worse still, she could never have explained her actions to Worthington.

They both felt a sense of relief when the Desk Nurse informed them that Dr. Kobler was ready. Abbie wheeled Brent down the hallway to the psychiatrist's office.

Abbie had imagined him as a wiry, gray-haired scientist with a monocle and goatee. In actuality, he was middle-aged, with dark hair, and nearly handsome. Brent's description of his disposition, however, had been spot-on.

Brent, ever the gentleman Worthington had raised him to be, made introductions. "Dr. Kobler, this is my girlfriend, Abigail Wentworth."

Kobler took her hand and greeted her politely, but no more than necessary. "Pleasure to meet you, Miss Wentworth."

Abbie immediately noted the disdain in his voice. Particularly when he turned back to Brent. "You'll find your mother outside on the grounds. She does enjoy the sunshine. If you prefer, I can have an orderly take you."

"That won't be necessary," Brent told him. "I know the way."

"Very well then," Dr. Kobler replied. "I have patients that require my attention. And please, tell Mr. Worthington that we would greatly enjoy his presence on your next visit."

THE LUSH, floral gardens of the hospital grounds were a welcome respite from the imposing, dark sterility of the main building. As soon as they were outside, Abbie asked, "What does he have against you?"

"You noticed?" Brent replied with the appropriate sarcasm.

"How could I not?" she asked.

"He much prefers speaking with Worthington," Brent explained as she pushed him past the tall bushes and assorted flower gardens. "He still sees me as a child. Bringing my girlfriend certainly didn't help."

"I can imagine," Abbie commented. She quickly glanced back to the main building, wondering if they were to be trusted on the grounds by themselves.

"I've tried to ask him about my mother's condition," Brent continued, "but he only wants to speak with Worthington. It's like pulling teeth trying to get any answers out of him."

Abbie wheeled him through the winding green gardens, each filled with lilies, orchids, carnations, and other foliage. They passed a few orderlies and the occasional nurse busy attending to other patients.

They finally reached Brent's mother, Sarah Gregor, in what had become her favorite spot. She was seated on a bench in the rose garden, enjoying the sunshine and tranquility of her surroundings.

Despite Brent's description of his mother's current state, Abbie had been unprepared for the full reality of her appearance. Gone was the kind, poised, elegant beauty she remembered from her childhood.

Instead, they encountered an aged, wild-eyed woman in a dark-gray hospital frock. Her once-beautiful Auburn hair was close-cropped with streaks of gray and a bald patch in the back from where the bullet had entered her skull.

Abbie instinctively took a step back.

Brent had to wheel himself closer to greet his mother. "Thomas?" Sarah Gregor asked softly as he approached.

"No, Mother. It's Brent," he explained.

She looked him over curiously before her eyes lit up with a spark of recognition. "Yes, Brent. I haven't seen you in ages, I think."

He reached over and took her hand. "I've been away at school, Mother. We're home for the summer."

She looked back at Brent with sad and pleading eyes. "Why won't you let me come home? You know I don't belong here."

Brent did his best to comfort her. "You know I can't do that, Mother. The doctors need to make you well first."

Sadly, both he and Abbie knew that day would never come. He couldn't help but notice her jagged nails. He later learned that she clawed at her door at night, trying to escape.

She looked up at Abbie and eyed her suspiciously. "And who is this you've brought?"

Brent motioned for Abbie to step closer. "Mother, this is Abigail. You remember her. She lives next door. We used to play together."

Sarah snapped at him angrily. "Is this why you keep me locked up in here? So you can fornicate with this trollop?"

Sarah let out a shriek and lunged at him. Brent toppled over in his chair. He just managed to catch her flailing arms as she tried desperately to claw at his face.

Abbie shouted to the nearby orderlies. "Help! Please!"

But they weren't close enough. She had to do something. Brent couldn't hold her off much longer.

Abbie grabbed the crazed woman by the shoulders and yanked her back.

Sarah immediately lashed back and clawed Abbie across the side of her face. The poor girl screamed and toppled over backwards into the grass.

Luckily, Brent was able to maneuver himself behind the still-toppled chair. It was just what they needed to prevent further injury. And just long enough for two burly orderlies to race over. It took both men to hold her down.

The kindly, middle-aged Nurse Hudson was right behind them. "Oh my heavens!" she exclaimed. She didn't know to which one to attend first.

Brent's only thought was of Abbie. He looked over to see her lying nearby, clutching the side of her face. Blood ran down and had dripped onto her blouse.

"Don't worry, we've got her," the Orderlies assured them.

They hurriedly carried Sarah Gregor away, kicking and screaming.

Nurse Hudson's instincts as a caretaker told her to first attend to the bleeding girl. But Abbie quickly got to her feet and insisted that she first help Brent back into his chair.

"Now we really must get that looked at," Nurse Hudson told Abbie.

"No," a distraught Abbie insisted. "I want to leave. Please Brent, I just want to go."

Had he been able to take her home himself, Brent would have readily agreed. But he was dependent on her to drive.

And she was clearly still too flustered to get behind the wheel.

NURSE HUDSON led them to the nurse's station in the main building. Abbie winced as the woman carefully wiped away the blood and cleaned the wound with iodine.

"I'm so sorry, Miss," Nurse Hudson told her. "If we'd known you were coming, we'd have put her in a straight jacket. I'm afraid she's had a few episodes lately."

That was news to Brent.

Of course, Dr. Kobler hadn't mentioned a word of it. And he never came to check on them, either. Brent heard later that he actually blamed them for the incident.

"This will keep it clean until you can go see your regular doctor," Nurse Hudson instructed as she bandaged Abbie's young face. "And I'm afraid you'll probably have to say goodbye to this blouse. Such a shame, it's so divine on you."

WITH ABBIE patched up and calmed down, they drove straight to Dr. Wellman's office. He examined the scratch and complimented Abbie on the care she'd received. He didn't even change the bandage.

"There might be a faint scar," he told her, "but once it completely heals, it should hardly be noticeable."

This was not unfamiliar. She'd touched the scars on Brent's back and felt where the bullets had passed through. And now, she thought, she'd have one of her own

She didn't say another word until after they'd made it back to her house. They managed to avoid the servants and took the elevator upstairs to her room.

Brent apologized again, sorry beyond words for what his his mother had done. He repeated that he had no idea that she'd become violent. No one had told him a thing.

"Please," Abbie finally answered, "don't ever ask me to go back there. I just can't do it."

"Never, I promise," he insisted. "Never again. I'm so sorry for the whole incident."

She sat there silently for the longest moment, then added, "Brent, I need you to promise me something else. Promise me *you'll* never go back there, either."

"But she's my mother," he protested.

"No, she isn't," Abbie insisted. "Not anymore."

Now it was Brent's turn to contemplate. Seeing her sitting there before him, her beautiful face damaged, and the brightness dimmed in her eyes. How could he not agree?

It was a promise he very nearly kept.

CHAPTER TEN

VICKY bounded down to the press room at City Hall. It felt strange to go back to her old haunt. Of course, nothing had changed, except for being mostly vacant.

"Hey, Morty, how's tricks?" she asked as she stepped in the door.

"Vicky!" Morty beamed when he turned around to see her. He gave her a big, comforting bear hug. "What'd ya know good?"

"Covering the big ceremony to-morrow," she told him. "Figured you'd still be here. Just thought I'd stop by and say hello."

He nodded in acknowledgment. "Of course, of course. Grab a seat."

"Where's Higgs?" she asked, curious, as she plopped down into her old chair. "Already gone home for the night?"

"Oh, you know, Bill," Morty explained as he glanced at his pocket watch. "He was out of here at 4:30. Likely sooner."

"Listen, you got a couple minutes?" she asked looking back, making sure that no one else was around.

"Sure," he replied in his usual fatherly tone. "What's on your mind, Kid?"

"What can you tell me about Flynn?" she asked.

"He's a decent enough guy," Morty said diplomatically. "Long career. Yeah, he takes a little on the side, but no more than anybody else. Why, you hear something?"

"Maybe," Vicky replied in a hushed tone. "That's what I'm trying to figure out. This whole incident with Nails just doesn't add up for me."

"Pretty suspicious, huh?" he chuckled with a nod to Higgs' empty chair. "Figured you were onto something."

"Well, so far I keep hitting a brick wall at every corner."

"You just be careful," he advised. "Flynn's getting a medal from the Mayor to-morrow. You want to watch who's feathers you ruffle."

"Come on, Morty. You know that's not exactly my style," Vicky replied as she got back up. "Gotta poke the hornet's nest."

"Well, good luck, Kid," Morty offered. "You just get ready to run when they come out."

Willie Potatoes and Tommy Clams strolled into The Grafton Public House. A cramped little dive that was always good for a stiff drink and a friendly ear. It was early yet and the place was still pretty quiet. Tommy hung by the door as Willie made his way to the bar.

Nick, the regular bartender, greeted him nervously. It wasn't yet Friday, so he was puzzled by the visit. But he wasn't about to tell them that.

"What'ya know, fellas?" Nick asked. "What can I get for you?"

Willie smiled at him and leaned against the bar. "You know who we are, right Nick?"

"Sure, Willie, of course," Nick replied. He had no idea where this was going and was understandably nervous about saying the wrong thing.

Willie continued, "And you know who we're looking for, right?"

So that's what this was about, Nick thought. He should have guessed.

"Look, Willie," Nick smiled nervously. "We don't want no trouble."

"You see, that's where we're in agreement," Willie replied as he grabbed a handful of peanuts. "You tell us where we can find him, and there won't be any."

VICKY pulled her small coupe up to the curb outside Officer Shayne's house. Though it was after dinner, it was a good hour before sundown. The neighborhood kids still out playing in the street.

The homes, all ten years old or more, were built exactly alike. Each was a long, narrow, single-story brick domicile with a small front porch and a tiny back yard. All very close together.

She was certain the neighbors had a difficult time telling them apart. Though she was equally sure they all felt an extra sense of security knowing there was a policeman on the block.

Vicky took off her jacket to appear more neighborly. Then strode up the walk, onto the porch, and knocked on the front door. Mrs. Shayne opened it shortly afterwards with a friendly smile. "Oh, hello?"

Vicky quickly sized her up as the type of woman completely beholden to her husband, who gave him the final word on all matters. Mrs. Shayne wore a simple dress and still kept her hair long, tied up in a sensible bun that made her look just a little older than her years.

Through the narrow house, Vicky could just barely spy the burly policeman seated in the kitchen, still dressed in the white shirt and dark blue pants of his crisp uniform. He nursed a cup of coffee and read the paper. There was no sign of any children, whom she assumed were outside, among the kids she'd seen down the street.

"Mrs. Shayne," Vicky introduced herself. "I'm a reporter for the *Daily Crusader*."

"Oh, my goodness, really?" Mrs. Shayne reacted in pleasant surprise. Vicky wasn't sure if that was because they weren't used to the press knocking on their door, or because a young woman like her was actually a reporter. She wanted to believe it was the former.

"I'm so terribly sorry to bother you at home," Vicky continued. "But I've been trying to talk to your husband and, well, it's just been difficult to catch up with him these last couple days."

"Well, it has been quite a whirlwind," Mrs. Shayne agreed, though her worried expression seemed to say so much more.

"If I could just have a few minutes of his time," Vicky implored.

"I'm so sorry," Mrs. Shayne informed her as she moved to close the door. "But he doesn't want to talk to anyone. He's very tired, as you can imagine. He's not feeling very well. Perhaps some other time."

To her credit, lying did not come naturally. Unlike Vicky, for whom it was just another part of the job.

"But he's a hero," Vicky protested. "I'm sure our readers would love to hear his side of the story."

"You have to understand," Mrs. Shayne shook her head apologetically. "He's just modest, that's all."

Vicky was sure something was wrong. But she also knew that if she just kept talking, Mrs. Shayne wouldn't close the door on her. Which was much more preferable than using her foot. And that if she were persistent enough, the little woman would have to appeal to her husband to get rid of her.

"Please," Vicky implored, "if you'd just let him know I'm here. "It won't take long. Promise."

Agnes Shayne stood silently for a moment and breathed a quiet sigh of frustration. Between the two of them, Vicky was clearly the more strong-willed. As much as she hated to admit it, there was no getting rid of this woman on her own.

"If you wouldn't mind," she finally relented. "Just wait right here."

"Thank you." Vicky watched from the porch as Mrs. Shayne stepped back and made her way to the kitchen. Agnes hesitated a moment longer before she interrupted her husband and pointed towards Vicky.

Vicky couldn't hear any of the conversation, but from what she could see, he wasn't at all happy about the situation. Mrs. Shayne stepped back as he threw down his paper and looked towards the door. Fortunately, he saved most of his aggravation for Vicky. He couldn't very well fault his wife for being too kind-hearted.

Officer Shayne barreled towards the door like a stung bull and jerked it open.

Vicky instinctively took a step back. His height coupled with his anger made for an imposing figure indeed. "What's this all about? he barked. "Didn't my wife already tell you I don't want to talk?"

His expression quickly changed when he saw that she was a woman. He backed down sheepishly. "Sorry, Miss. Thought you were another one of those bloodhounds."

Then just as suddenly, it changed yet again when he recognized her. "Say, I already talked to you at the hospital —"

Vicky realized that, at this point, kindness was still her greatest weapon. "I'm so sorry to barge in on you like this," she offered apologetically. "But please, Officer, I just want to ask you a few more questions."

Shayne shuffled a moment as he mulled the thought, then finally blurted, "I already said all I'm gonna say. Now please, just leave us alone."

And with that, he closed the door on her.

Vicky stood there a moment and thought about knocking again. But it was no use. Another brick wall. Something she should be getting used to, she thought.

Despite the lack of answers, one thing was perfectly clear.

Officer Shayne didn't sound like a man who was about to get honored by the Mayor in front of his family and the entire city.

CHAPTER ELEVEN

WORTHINGTON checked his pocket watch as he stepped down from the Gregor family's private rail car onto the platform at Union Station. He was pleased to see that they had actually arrived a good ten minutes before their scheduled time of 2:05 in the afternoon.

He was even more pleased that there wasn't a single reporter in sight. Least of all Leonore Lamonte, whom he hoped was still back in Los Angeles.

He was well aware (Master Gregor less so) of the tumultuous events that had transpired since they'd traveled across the country less than a week earlier. The police shooting of Irish gangster James McCarthy, his miraculous survival, and subsequent arrest. All of which had culminated in the grand awards ceremony that afternoon to honor the officers involved.

Which, in a well-timed coincidence, happened to take place at the same hour as their arrival.

Worthington was equally pleased to be greeted by their usual porter. Walter Rawlins was a spry, middle-aged negro man who was equally fit in both mind and body. With him was his teenage son, Raymond, who'd already surpassed his father in height. With more accomplishments yet to come.

The Rawlins family, like most negroes in town, lived in the South Side neighborhood of Arlington Park. But most in Terminal City just called it "Bronzeville." Despite being deep in Big Jack's territory, it was one neighborhood he didn't touch. Like Chinatown on the North Side, they had their own criminal element which operated without interference. They even had their own newspaper, *The Evening Hubbub*, an entertaining 8-page rag that covered the local nightlife.

"Good afternoon, Mr. Worthington," Walter greeted him happily. "Welcome home. So good to see you, Sir."

Worthington looked back at them in astonishment. Both men stood tall in their dark blue porter uniforms with shiny gold buttons. "Oh, my heavens! Is this little Raymond?"

"Not so little anymore, is he?" Walter beamed proudly. "He's just working with me for the summer. Then heading off to college come September."

"And law school after that," Raymond added. Worthington was even more surprised by how deep the young man's voice had gotten.

Raymond reached out and shook the older man's hand vigorously. "Good to see you again, Mr. Worthington. I just wanted to thank Mr. Gregor for his wonderful generosity."

Before Worthington could respond, Walter quickly added, "Don't worry, he knows not to say anything. I already told him how shy Mr. Gregor is about such things."

Worthington offered a relieved smile. For the truth was, Brent was only *partially* aware of his private generosity towards the underprivileged in Terminal City. Deep down he had a warm heart, but was, unfortunately, always too consumed with his own needs to see those of others. However, Worthington had convinced him years earlier to offer a sizable portion of his income to charitable causes. Brent had readily agreed to this, with Worthington given full discretion on how it was to be administered.

"I'll go get your luggage, Sir," Raymond offered enthusiastically. "We've got the car already waiting."

Both men watched proudly as the young man bounded down the platform to the opposite end. Once he was gone, Worthington discreetly pulled Walter aside and spoke in hushed tones. "Regarding Master Gregor, I'm afraid I must appeal to your greater discretion once again."

MAYOR EUGENE BARKER proudly took the stage in the Kennelly Band Shell (modeled after the Hollywood Bowl), which had been built two years earlier at the south end of Harrison Park. It's completion had been in question until Margeaux Kennelly, a great lover of music and the beautiful French wife of Julius Kennelly, had convinced her husband to donate much of the needed funds.

Barker delivered a rousing speech "to honor two brave men who proudly represent what it means to be called *our city's finest.*" His voice echoed through the loudspeakers and could be heard for blocks on end. For those residents who somehow couldn't hear it, the ceremony was also broadcast live on the radio.

With him were guests of honor Detective Sergeant Michael Flynn and Officer Robert Shayne. The two men wore their dress uniforms and were accompanied by their families. Also on stage were Chief Harry LaSalle, District Attorney Doc Milford, several aldermen from the City Council, and the Terminal City Marching Band. Who punctuated Barker's speech with numerous drum licks and cymbal crashes.

Vicky watched this circus from the press box below. Despite having already downed an extra dose of pain killers, the noise level *did wonders* for her ever-present headache. Which should have caused her to have second thoughts about any grandstanding.

Every other reporter in town was there covering the event, including Lyons (who looked reasonably sober), Morty, Higgs, Charlie, and Gelbart. Even Leonore was there, though she wouldn't have been caught dead anywhere near the press box. Instead, she was too busy hobnobbing with the Kennellys and other blue bloods in attendance.

Frank was actually there, too, but he was in the crowd with Betty and the girls. Which was a shame because, had he been closer to the press box, he might have been able to stop what was about to happen before it was too late.

"And now," Barker concluded, "I invite Chief LaSalle up to the stage to help me present the awards."

LaSalle joined him and took the microphone. He'd been itching to get center stage. He smiled proudly and was bathed in the usual sea of flashbulbs.

"Thank you Mayor Barker, Gentlemen of the City Council, and especially to all of you good people of Terminal City," LaSalle began. "It is my great and humble honor to serve as your Chief of Police. It is an even greater honor, however, to recognize these two fine men. They are both a credit to the Department. And to their Country. Detective Sergeant Flynn? Officer Shayne? Will you join me, please?"

Flynn and Shayne both stepped up to center stage and saluted the Chief. Flynn was accompanied by his wife, Ethel. The pristine white cloth of his sling practically glowed against the blue of his dress uniform.

Vicky remarked to Morty, "Surprised he's not still in the wheelchair." To which she heard Higgs actually snicker.

Shayne was accompanied by Agnes and Bobby Junior. Vicky couldn't tell who was more uncomfortable between the parents. Shayne was quiet and stiff. Agnes was bashful and fidgety. Bobby Junior was the only one excited to be on stage.

"Detective Flynn, Officer Shayne," LaSalle announced. "I think I speak for the entire city when I offer my most sincere thanks to both of you for your unwavering dedication and incredible bravery."

The band provided a drum roll as LaSalle pinned the medals, first to Flynn's coat (which already had several) and then to Shayne's (which only had one). A cymbal clash signaled the crowd to break out into applause.

LaSalle shook their hands and continued, "Officer Shayne, it is my distinct honor to hereby promote you to the rank of Detective."

Shayne stepped back in surprise. He practically had to catch Agnes before she went weak in the knees.

LaSalle waited for the applause to die down before he concluded. "Detective Sergeant Flynn, it is my distinct honor to hereby promote you to the rank of Detective Lieutenant. Congratulations to both of you! Well deserved, Men!"

"Well, isn't this a fine how-do-you-do?" Vicky remarked.

Mayor Barker shook their hands vigorously. Ethel Flynn was clearly used to the pomp and circumstance, but Agnes

Shayne was close to needing smelling salts. Bobby Junior was about to burst with excitement.

Mayor Barker knelt down to the boy. "Tell me, Son, are you proud of your father?"

"You're darn right I am!" Bobby Junior shouted. "When I grow up, I want to be a G-Man! So I can hunt down gangsters just like my Dad!"

Then he imitated using a tommy gun on the whole crowd, sound effects and all.

"Junior!" Agnes exclaimed. That got her to speak up. She quickly pulled him back to her side.

"That's the spirit, young man!" Mayor Barker chuckled. "And now we'd like to take a few questions from the loyal members of the press."

LaSalle and Flynn fielded one softball question after another and took turns with Flynn to answer. All of which were met with cheers and laughter from the crowd.

"Detective Flynn, were you scared going up against a dangerous gangster like Nails McCarthy? Chief LaSalle, what's it like to have such heroic men working in your department? Detective Flynn, did you frame the bullet?"

On the rare occasion that Shayne actually got a question, he replied with just a one-word answer. And looked increasingly more uncomfortable with each passing minute.

As expected, LaSalle managed to skip over Vicky each time. The frustration only made her headache worse.

"Officer Shayne, were you surprised by the promotion? Detective Flynn, when will you go back to work? Any word on a date for the trial? Officer Shayne, what's it like to be such a great hero?"

Finally, she just shouted it out. "Is it true that Nails McCarthy was unarmed?"

That got their attention.

Mayor Barker stormed to the microphone. "How did you get in here, Miss?"

Barker was offended that anyone would even insinuate such a horrible idea. And coming from the mouth of a woman at that. "Next question!"

But Flynn knew better than to just ignore it. "No, the lady asked a question, and we're here to answer. What's your name again, Miss?" As if he didn't already know.

"Vicky Rose, *Daily Crusader*."

"And where did you hear this?" he asked politely.

"I have my sources," she retorted, trying to egg him into an admission.

It wasn't exactly working. "Young lady, my good mother always taught me to respect the fairer sex. Are you actually suggesting that James McCarthy was *unarmed* at the time of his arrest?"

A murmur rippled through the assembled crowd, punctuated by a symphony of flashbulbs.

Lyons couldn't help but chuckle to himself. *Now she's really stepped in it*, he thought. *Just might get rid of her for good.*

Leonore shared the sentiment from her spot with the Kennellys. She just shook her head and smiled with satisfaction.

Frank felt his heart sink. He knew this wouldn't end well. "I'll be right back," he told Betty then pushed his way towards the press box.

Morty gave Lyons a forceful nudge. "Help her out, Chester!"

Lyons just smirked back. "She's a big girl. She can't take it, then she ought'n even be here."

"And are you, therefore, insinuating that I wasn't actually shot in the altercation?" Flynn continued. "I can assure you that my wounds are real. Would you like to step up and see for yourself?"

The crowd chuckled at Vicky's expense. But she wasn't about to back down just yet. "No," she replied, doing her best to defend herself. "I'm not suggesting that you weren't shot."

"Well, how did it happen then?" he retorted.

Morty wanted to help her, but it was too late. The ball had already started rolling. He thought his best bet was to throw out another question they didn't want to answer. "Any luck finding Whitey O'Leary?" Morty shouted.

"No, no," Flynn replied cheerfully. "We'll come back to you, Morty. But first, I want to answer the little lady here. Tell me, Miss. Did one of the other men shoot me from the other room? After they had all been disarmed and apprehended?"

Vicky just stood silently.

"No, of course not," he continued. "Did Officer Shayne shoot me? The very man who stands up here with me being honored by the Mayor?"

Again, Vicky stood silent. Flynn turned to Shayne.

"Officer Shayne, did you shoot me while we were arresting Nails McCarthy?"

Shayne stood motionless, still clearly uncomfortable. Vicky thought for just a moment that he might say something in her defense. But he just shook his head, his expression unchanged. "No, Sir."

"Well then," Flynn smiled, having succeeded in making a mockery of her. "I think we can only draw one conclusion. I must have shot myself!" The crowd erupted in laughter. Vicky noticed Shayne look away.

"Poor kid," Morty commented. For once, Higgs had nothing to say. He, too, just shook his head in disgust.

Flynn played his mockery to the hilt and presented his good hand to Shayne. "Officer Shayne, I order you to arrest me for assaulting a police officer!"

The crowd laughed. Lyons laughed right along with them. *Poor kid got what she deserved*, he thought.

"I'd offer you both, but as you can see, my other arm is in a sling!"

Vicky felt pretty foolish. She'd been left with egg all over her face. And in front of the entire city, no less.

Frank finally reached the press box and put an arm on her shoulder. She buried her face in her hands. Frank gave Lyons a disappointed look, but the older reporter simply shrugged.

"Come on, Red," he consoled her. "I'll take you back to the office."

"Thanks," she sniffled, then thought the better of it.

"Actually, you mind dropping me off at the Carousel instead?"

WORTHINGTON had the full staff line up in the grand foyer for inspection. He couldn't help but notice how much their numbers had dwindled over the years. But with only Master Gregor and himself, they could have done with fewer still. And likely would at some point.

At the head of the line was Mr. Coleman, a middle-aged negro man who'd been employed with the Gregors since Nate Gregor had built the house some 26 years earlier. As the cook and second only to Worthington, Mr. Coleman was the only remaining member of the once-larger kitchen staff.

Next was Mr. Donaldson, a white-haired former police captain. He was a tough old Irishman who, given the chance, could show those gangsters, like Nails and Whitey, a thing or two. He'd been with the Gregors for fifteen years, since shortly after that fateful Halloween night when his position had become necessary.

Third was Mr. Olmstead, a wiry, bearded man whom the others rarely saw inside the house. He maintained the grounds and during the summer would supervise a handful of carefully-vetted (by Mr. Donaldson) assistants.

Lastly were Mrs. Poole and her small cadre of housekeepers, Elyse, Mollie, and young Bridget. Mrs. Sally Poole had also been there that on that fateful Halloween, having been hired only a few years after Mr. Coleman. In her time working for the Gregors, she'd gotten married, had children of her own, and even her first grandchild.

Under normal circumstances, they would have all been there to greet Master Gregor upon his arrival. But on this occasion, due to Master Gregor's *condition*, Mr. Coleman and Mr. Donaldson had already assisted in getting the young head of the house upstairs.

Worthington had planned to do a formal inspection. But considering the hour (most of the staff were due to go home) and the circumstances, he thought the better of it.

"I should like to thank each of you for your dedication while we were away," Worthington stated. "Unfortunately, Master Gregor is not feeling well, and requires a few days' rest."

While the entire staff was well aware of the actual situation by this point, they displayed the appropriate concern. And knew also to exercise the appropriate discretion.

"With that in mind," Worthington continued, "I should like to forgo the usual inspection until the morrow."

This announcement was not exactly met with elation. With the following day being Sunday, the majority of the staff had the day off.

"Not to worry, however," Worthington reassured them. "For those of you not scheduled to be here, I shall not ask you to come in. We shall make due with whomever is on board. Again, I thank you, and do have a good night."

That was much better received.

KID YELLOW limped out of the corner liquor store. It was getting late, but he was only a few blocks from the hotel where he was hiding out. He usually hung out at The Grafton, but he'd already been tipped off that Willie Potatoes was out looking for him. Best to keep low for awhile till things died down.

He quickly peered out of the doorway and looked around. Coast was clear. He wasn't the fastest man, so he had to be extra careful.

He'd only gotten a block and a half when he heard a car approach from behind. He tried to duck into a doorway, but he was too slow. The car pulled up to the curb. "Looks like you could use a lift."

Kid Yellow looked up to see Willie Potatoes. With his arm in a sling, Willie looked less intimidating. Someone Kid Yellow could easily outrun. But Willie would never travel alone. Tommy Clams and Fingers Scarrone were right behind him, waiting in the shadows. Just as he thought.

Yellow looked around. He was a sitting duck. He reached for his gun as Tommy and Fingers reached for theirs. Willie just shook his head.

"Come on, Yellow," he implored. "You don't want to die out here on the sidewalk, do ya?"

Yellow quickly mulled it over. As much as he wanted to gun them all down right there, he knew he was slower on the draw, too.

Yellow offered a friendly smile. "Come on, fellas, what'dya want with me, anyways? I'm just a little guy. They don't tell me nothing."

"Lookit," Willie entreated, "we just want to have a little chat is all. Ask a few questions. Get in the car. Save you some walking."

They had him surrounded. If he were to have any chance of living, he had to do exactly as they said.

WITH THE staff gone for the night, Worthington had one room inspection that simply could not wait. After checking to make sure that Master Gregor was fast asleep, he quietly made his way downstairs.

He passed the suit of armor and quickly retrieving the key from his coat pocket, he checked the study door. As he'd hoped, it was still locked. Then he quietly opened it and went in.

Worthington well knew that to the maids and others the grand house was known as "the Murder Mansion." Less frightening than the Patterson house (to his knowledge, there were no Halloween rituals performed by the neighborhood children), but certainly just as notorious.

Had Brent been older, they might have opted to move elsewhere. But he was young and despite its large size, the house met his physical requirements by having an elevator and ramps constructed for his wheelchair.

So Worthington just closed the room off. And Master Gregor vowed never to go in there again.

For five years it was never cleaned or dusted. That was until young Brent, at age 15, became interested in a local disappearance. And he needed his father's files to work the case on his own. Unable to enter the study, he sent Worthington down to retrieve them.

Since then, Worthington had kept the room clean himself. Going in at least once a month, always out of sight of his charge and employer.

He hoped that one day Master Gregor might face his fears and re-open the room. But for that to happen, he'd need a more pressing reason than obtaining his father's files.

And what reason that might be, Worthington had no idea.

DR. EUGENE TUNG locked up his spare, two-room office, ready to leave for the night. He was a middle-aged man with receding black hair and round, wire-rimmed glasses. He'd lived in the United States for much of his life and had almost no discernible accent. Most of his patients were in Chinatown, and he'd always helped the Parish there whenever he could.

His practice was on the second floor of the Han Leong Chinese Merchants Association Building. It was more commonly known around town as "Chinese City Hall." With its Oriental features and tall pagodas that anchored each front corner, it was easily the most prominent building in Chinatown. And much of Terminal City, for that matter.

The Association was run by Sam Yuen, head of the Four Brothers Tong, which had ties to Vito Spats and the Mob. The Tong ran most of the neighborhood brothels and opium dens. Though it was never an ideal relationship for Dr. Tung or the Chinatown Parish, they certainly benefited from being under Yuen's watchful eye. The elderly Tong leader was very protective of his tenants.

Dr. Tung had just reached the stairs when he ran into another party on their way up. At the front was Yo Hing, a flashy young gangster who worked for Yuen. With him were two men he didn't recognize, but didn't have to. Willie Potatoes and Tommy Clams.

The Doctor immediately stepped aside with his head bowed to let the group pass. He knew he was safe under Sam Yuen's protection, but always showed deference just to be careful. Especially with regard to outsiders.

Yo Hing bowed and greeted him cordially. "Afternoon, Doctor."

Willie stopped short on the stairs. A smile broke across his face. "What'd you know, a Chinaman doctor!" Willie let out a laugh and patted the physician on the shoulder before continuing up the next flight.

Dr. Tung said nothing. He just waited for the men to reach the next landing before heading down himself.

As he was about to go, he overheard Willie express concern about being seen. Yo Hing assured him not to worry. He knew Dr. Tung could be trusted.

The Chinese were very good at keeping secrets.

JERRY watched with surprise as Vicky gulped down her double chocolate. Most people went to a bar to drown their sorrows. Vicky came to his ice cream parlor.

But that wasn't the part that surprised him. It was when she chased it with four of the biggest horse pills he'd ever seen anyone, dame or otherwise, choke down. *That was a first*, he thought. "How many of those things are you taking?" he asked.

"Not enough," Vicky replied, touching her forehead.

"Maybe you should see a doctor," Jerry suggested with deep concern.

"I did," she replied, and took another big sip.

"A real doctor?" he had to ask, picking up her pill bottle. "I've seen smaller pills from a veterinarian."

"Real enough," she told him and took another sip. "Why does everyone keep asking me that?"

"Just worry about you is all," he told her.

Time to change the subject. "So, you listen to the radio lately?" she asked and chugged back the last of it.

"Yep, afraid so. Heard the whole thing." Jerry did his best to console her. "Ever tell you about the time my plane was on fire, I was going down, and I didn't have a parachute?"

"Yeah," she replied. "But maybe you need to tell me again. And while you're at it, you can mix me another."

Jerry took the empty glass and watched as she closed her eyes and rubbed her forehead. "Why don't you go home and get some rest?" he suggested. "Just take it easy to-morrow. Relax with that new boyfriend of yours."

She had to chuckle at that one. Spending time with Denny wasn't exactly her idea of relaxation. "Don't you worry about me, Jerry," she assured him. "I'll be just fine."

She never even noticed the car parked across the street.

CHAPTER TWELVE

VICKY stirred awake, groggy, her vision blurred. Surprisingly, her head wasn't pounding like it normally did in the morning. Though she did feel unusually dizzy. She wondered if she'd taken too many pills the night before. But honestly, she couldn't remember. She didn't even remember going home.

She wondered, too, what time it was. She reached for her alarm clock, but it wasn't there. That's when she began to realize that she wasn't actually in her bedroom.

She wasn't even in her own apartment.

The last thing she remembered was being at the Carousel with Jerry.

"Jerry?" she asked hazily as she struggled to open her eyes.

Then she saw that she was dressed in a patient gown. And that she'd woken up in the hospital.

"Jerry?" she called out again, confused. She had no idea if he was there. He was just the last person she remembered seeing.

Frank stirred from the chair. From the looks of him, even through her blurred vision, he looked a mess.

"Frank, what the hell?" she called out. "Where am I? Where's Jerry?" She tried to get out of the hospital bed.

Frank stumbled to his feet just in time to stop her. "Calm down, Red. It's okay," he reassured her. "You're gonna be just fine."

"But how'd I get here?" she asked.

"You blacked out," he explained. "Your buddy down at

the Carousel found you just sitting in your car when he closed up. Said you'd been out there a good hour. So he called me."

Vicky rubbed her head. Thankfully, her headache was gone for a change. But it had been replaced by dizziness and nausea.

Frank helped her lie back down. "Listen, Red," he implored. "It's time you saw a real doctor. Somebody better than that old guy who gave you those horse pills."

"But I love Doctor Murphy," she protested.

"The Doc here says he wants to do some x-rays. No telling what they did to you back at that asylum. Was thinking we should call your family, let somebody know what's going on."

"I don't have time for this, Frank," she protested. "I'm telling you, I'll be just fine."

"Look," he stopped her. "You don't have to prove to me that you're cut out for the job. You've already done that. The story can wait."

That one threw Vicky for a loop. In all the time she'd known Frank, the story had *always* come first. That's when she realized he was truly concerned.

"Let's just get those x-rays and see what the doctor says, okay?" he insisted.

"Okay," she nodded, then realized he was still wearing the same clothes from the day before. "You been here all night?"

"Yeah, of course," he replied. "No big deal. Soon as Betty and the girls get out of church, they're bringing me some fresh rags. Maybe by then we'll know something."

That's when Vicky started to realize what it was like to have a good father.

BRENT GREGOR struggled to wake. After a long journey home, he was somewhat relieved to find himself in his own bed. But on this occasion, it gave him neither comfort nor satisfaction.

He quickly reached for the bell on the night stand and rang it furiously. The sound echoed in his own ears, and he stopped just as quickly.

Moments later, following hurried footsteps in the hall, he heard a young woman's tentative voice at the door. "Are you quite all right, Sir? Can I get you anything?"

"I can't hear you out there," he commanded as he sat up and worked to clear his head. "Come in here."

Elyse stepped in just barely, careful to avert her eyes.

"Don't worry," he told her. "I'm presentable enough." Then he quickly checked the covers and beneath to make sure he was being truthful. He had little-to-no memory of getting in his pajamas. Much less going to bed.

She stepped further in and, with her head low, demurred, preferring to ask again, "May I get you anything, Master Gregor? Some breakfast perhaps?"

"Where's Worthington?" Brent asked, still in a fog.

"He's at church, Sir," she answered politely. "He didn't want to go, but I assured him I would look after you. Should be back soon enough."

He sat there silent and still for several moments, to the point where she wondered if he had fallen back asleep. "Yes, some breakfast please," he finally responded.

"Very well, Sir," she curtsied. "I'll have it up for you shortly. Until then, there's a glass of water and aspirin on the night stand."

He was sure he didn't remember seeing those. But when he turned to look, there they were. "Thank you..." he offered, then his voice simply trailed off as he struggled to remember her name.

"It's Elyse, Sir," she politely reminded him as she backed towards the door. "And you're most welcome."

DOCTOR LEVINE switched on the large, wooden radiograph viewer and turned out the light in his lab. Three x-rays of Vicky's head were mounted on the top row. Levine was a pudgy, balding man with wire glasses and a friendly demeanor. He immediately turned to Frank.

"Now, if you'll look here, Mr. Rose," he began to explain.

"No no," Vicky quickly corrected him, stepping in front of Frank. "He's not Mr. Rose, he's my boss."

"As it should be, Miss," Dr. Levine answered with an approving smile.

"No, he's not my husband," she tried again to explain. "He's just my *employer*."

"I see," Dr. Levine replied with a clear wink in his voice. "Well then, do you have any other family that you can call?"

Vicky just shrugged in exasperation. Denny was the closest she had to a significant other. And she wasn't about to call him. "Not here," she said. I live alone."

It sounded so pathetic (final? permanent?) when she said it aloud.

Dr. Levine stood there awkwardly for a moment, unsure of what to say next. He finally just addressed his comments to no one in particular. "Now, if you'll look here, this is very curious."

He drew his fingers along a pair of shadows towards the top and back of her head. "There are four slight burn marks on her skull, as well as some scarring beneath her hairline."

He paused momentarily and searched for just the right words to approach such a delicate topic. "Pardon me for asking, but has she had any recent *psychiatric* treatment?"

"Something like that," commented Frank with dissatisfaction. He didn't feel he was at liberty to say more.

Vicky knew exactly what he was thinking. She closed her eyes and sighed in frustration. This was not the kind of news she wanted to hear. Especially in front of Frank.

"A fews weeks ago," Vicky explained. "Did a story down at the Asylum. It was an accident."

"And a very unfortunate one at that," Dr. Levine commented.

"Is she going to be okay, Doc?" Frank asked, the worry very clear in his voice.

"Fortunately," Levine explained, "the X-rays don't show anything too far out of the ordinary. But after reviewing all of the diagnoses at hand, I wish to keep her here another day or two for observation."

He checked her eyes with a small flashlight, moving it side to side to see how her pupils reacted. "Afterwards, I very strongly recommend that she take some time off. Get plenty of rest. I'll prescribe some different medication. Then have her come back and see me in two weeks."

"Two weeks?" Vicky shouted. "I can't take off for two weeks! I've got a major story I'm chasing."

"I'm afraid the alternative could be quite catastrophic," Dr. Levine added. "I'd say two weeks at a minimum. Then we can take another look and see if you're ready to go back to work."

This time, Vicky was more than happy to defer to Matson's judgment. "Frank, please tell him!"

"I'm not your husband," he replied firmly. "But the Doc says two weeks, so you're grounded for two weeks."

"But Frank..." she begged.

"You want to make it longer?" he asked.

WORTHINGTON checked his watch as he hustled down the second floor hallway. Still dressed in his Sunday finest with a newspaper under his arm, he'd just returned from church. He had debated not going at all. But Elyse had assured him that she would look after Master Gregor. And this was a time when prayer was sorely needed.

And there was every possibility that Brent would have slept the entire time.

Worthington peered in the doorway of the master bedroom and was surprised to find Brent sitting up. Not unsurprising, however, he was still in his bedclothes, his breakfast untouched.

He appeared lost in thought, his gaze fixed out the window where the Wentworth Mansion was just visible over the trees. Also not unexpected.

"Shall I clean this up for you, Sir?" Worthington asked, giving Brent a bit of a start. He hadn't heard the older gentleman enter.

"No, you go on to church," Brent sighed. "Don't worry about me."

"I've actually just returned, Sir," Worthington explained.

Brent offered no reaction.

"Very well then, Sir," Worthington continued. "I'll send Elyse up to see to it later."

Again, Brent offered no reaction.

"Would you care for the morning paper, Sir?"

Brent remained silent, lost in thought. Just staring out

the window.

Worthington set the paper on the bed within arm's reach. "I'll just go change then, Sir. I'll check in on you again shortly."

Brent still didn't answer.

DENNY rushed into the hospital lobby and straight to the front desk. Despite the large bouquet of flowers in his hand and the general brightness of his surroundings, it still made him nervous. The place reminded him too much of the incident at the Asylum just a few weeks before.

"Excuse me," he anxiously asked the middle-aged Desk Nurse, "I'm here to see Victoria Rose. Could you tell me which room she's in?"

The Nurse took one look at the bouquet and gave him an approving smile. "You must be the boyfriend."

"Uh, yes," Denny answered with some degree of uncertainty, not being entirely convinced himself. "Yes, yes I am. Denny Morris."

The Desk Nurse looked down at her records. "Let's see, she's in room 325. The elevator is just down the hall."

Denny quickly thanked her and was just about to dash off when the Nurse stopped him. "Actually, we didn't get all of her information when she checked in. I wonder if I might ask a few questions?"

"Of course," Denny replied, though he wasn't sure if he knew all the answers.

"Does she have any family?"

"Let's see," he thought, having just asked those same questions himself. "She has a mother and father, of course. Oh, and a brother and a sister."

"Would you happen to know their names?" she asked.

"No, I don't," Denny replied, feeling just a little embarrassed. Not wanting to sound completely ignorant, he then blurted out, "But I do know that her father and brother work in a bank, and her mother and sister are both schoolteachers."

"And do they live here?" the Nurse asked.

"No," Denny replied, feeling himself come up short again. He grew increasingly frustrated by how little he knew.

"Address?"

For that one, he could only manage one word.

"Missouri."

THE LAST thing Brent wanted to do was leave his room. But everywhere he looked, he was plagued by memories of Abbie. She was too much a part of his life to be so easily forgotten.

The hours that they'd spent there together on their own when Worthington had gone back to England. The time she had landed her plane on the front lawn. And he always saw her house any time he looked out the window. How much he had loved that before. And now it was an image that taunted him daily.

Brent picked up the paper that Worthington had left for him. It was the *Daily Crusader*.

At least that brought a more pleasant thought to his mind. How that reporter, Vicky Rose, had tried to sneak into his house disguised as a nurse. Perhaps not a more pleasant thought, but at least something to take his mind away.

At least he'd exposed her before she'd stuck him with that needle. And he had helped her save that man's life. And then rescued her from the Asylum. And faced Ned Vogel.

Again, not the most pleasant of memories.

He perused the front page. The headline screamed "HERO COPS HONORED BY MAYOR." So, that's why there was no one at the train station.

It wasn't her byline. Instead it was by Chester Lyons. He'd seen the name plenty of times before. Even as far back as the night Ned Vogel had broken into their house.

Yet again, not the most pleasant of memories.

The other headlines (some by Vicky Rose) were all about the Mob. Nails McCarthy's condition and arrest. Whitey O'Leary still on the run. Big Jack Torrissimo opening a new club, The Four Diamonds.

You can't pick up a paper without reading a story about the underworld, he thought to himself. *This whole city is going to hell.*

And it's all because of the Mob.

CHAPTER THIRTEEN

VICKY looked down the hospital hallway and made sure the coast was clear. Luckily, there wasn't a single doctor or nurse in sight. Which was actually no luck at all. She'd carefully noted the shift changes and knew just when to make her move.

Thankfully, Frank had left her a copy of the morning edition. And there on the front page was an article by her favorite journalist, Chester Lyons. Who'd dutifully provided an update on the condition of Nails McCarthy. Who, of course, was still in the hospital.

Which just so happened to be the very same one where she was.

What better way to try and see him, she thought, *than as a fellow patient?*

No one would look twice at her walking down the hall. This would be even better than that night at the prison. Had she realized this sooner, she'd have faked it.

Her headaches were finally working in her favor.

ELYSE stood by and watched as Worthington completed his inspection of the kitchen. She had no reason to be anxious. After all, the kitchen was in no way her responsibility (though she did occasionally serve). But most of all, because Mr. Coleman had never once failed an inspection.

The laundry would be a different story.

Because this was his one day off for the week, Mr. Coleman was not there. It made him nervous to have his kitchen inspected without his being present, and he'd even offered to come in.

But Worthington stayed true to his word and told him that it wasn't necessary. Besides, he had no doubt that Mr. Coleman's kitchen would remain the high-water mark against which all of the other rooms would be measured.

Worthington systematically went through each of the pantries, verified their contents, and that only the freshest of ingredients were being stored.

Next he went through the cupboards and inspected the silver, the glassware, and utensils. Not a single smudge or water spot was to be found.

Finally, he checked all the pots, pans, and counters. And just as he'd expected there, too, every little detail added up to perfection.

"Please inform Mr. Coleman that he has once again exceeded expectations," Worthington gladly proclaimed.

"Yes, Sir," Elyse curtsied. Of course, she well knew that this instruction was futile. Worthington would gladly pass on the news himself before she could do so.

DENNY knocked on the outside of Vicky's hospital room to alert his arrival. He was there with a ready smile and the bouquet he'd been carrying all morning. Even though the door was open, he wanted to make sure it was appropriate to enter. She'd already gotten on him more than once for overstepping his bounds.

He'd worried she might feel the same way about the hospital visit and had debated not going. But what kind of boyfriend would he be for not doing so?

But what bothered him even more was why she was there in the first place. He'd noticed the headaches and especially the medication she was taking. But he had no idea it had gotten that serious.

After knocking a second time and still getting no answer, he finally threw propriety to the wind and peaked in the doorway. And it was just as he'd feared.

Her bed was empty.

A quick check of the room confirmed his suspicions. Vicky was gone. But where?

Maybe just for a walk, he reasoned. Or even down to radiology to look at her X-rays. That seemed more than likely. But it didn't exactly seem like Vicky.

Denny stepped back out into the hall and looked around. Still no sign of her.

He went down to the Nurse's station and inquired. There he found Nurse Olivia, a motherly woman with a friendly demeanor. "Nurse," Denny inquired. "do you know where Miss Rose is?"

One look at Denny was all she needed to size him up. If nothing else, the earnest expression and giant bouquet were dead give-ways. "Oh, you must be the boyfriend."

"Yes, yes I am," he answered proudly. It was nice to be recognized in that capacity, even if it wasn't by Vicky herself.

"She's not in her room?" she asked curiously.

"No, ma'am, she's not."

"Did you check the lavatory?"

"Of course not," he blushed, "but the door was open, so..." He couldn't bring himself to get more specific.

"That gal was just in there a minute ago," she informed him. "You just wait right here."

Nurse Olivia got up and went to check the room for herself. Only moments later, she returned with a perplexed look on her face. "Now where in the devil could she have gotten off to?"

Denny stood there silently for a moment, just as confused. And even more, worried. He'd never anticipated that she wouldn't be there when he arrived. Or that the Nurses wouldn't even know that she was missing.

And that's when it hit him. "Excuse me, Nurse. But which way is Nails McCarthy's room?"

ELYSE and Bridget watched with grave anticipation as Worthington inspected the laundry. Again, Elyse had the comfort in knowing that this was not her full responsibility. Any blame to be had would be directed squarely at Mrs. Poole.

But if Elyse ever hoped for the job herself, she had to be absolutely diligent in making sure that, just like the kitchen, the laundry also exceeded expectations.

Worthington examined the washers, the drying racks, the sinks, and the folds on all the linens. The occasional "hmmm" of disapproval told them all that they needed to know.

"Well then," Worthington concluded, "this room more-or-less meets expectations." Which was to say that it didn't. "I shall have to discuss my notes with Mrs. Poole when she returns."

"Yes, of course, Sir," Elyse replied politely. Since she had to follow Worthington for the entire inspection, it was best to agree and just move on.

Bridget, on the other hand, was perfectly free to speak up. Only it wasn't at all about the laundry or his assessment.

"Is Master Gregor going to be okay?" she asked thoughtfully.

Worthington looked at her with pleasant surprise. "Yes, Bridget. I do hope so."

VICKY peered down the hallway towards Nails McCarthy's room. The only people milling about were the occasional nurse and other patients. There was a lone Police Officer on guard, but he was at the Nurse's Station chatting up the young ladies there.

Seeing her opportunity, Vicky rounded the corner and casually walked down the hall. Just as she hoped, in her hospital gown and her hair disheveled, she blended right in. She walked right past the Nurse's Station and the Policeman. No one paid her any mind.

Then she walked right into Nails McCarthy's room.

She'd been so focused on actually getting in there, she hadn't given much thought to what she'd find when she did. It shouldn't have taken her by surprise, but it did.

The Irish gangster was in bed, motionless, with the top half of his body covered in bandages. His head, his arm, and his torso completely immobilized. His face was mostly obscured, and were it not for the presence of a guard and the extent of his injuries, she couldn't have been sure it was even him.

She went to over his bed and sat down beside him. A

morphine drip ran down into his arm. He was barely conscious. "Mr. McCarthy," she spoke softly. "I need to ask you a question."

He looked up groggily to see a beautiful, Auburn-haired woman staring back at him. He couldn't be sure if she was a nurse or an angel. "What?" he answered groggily.

"Is it true you were unarmed when Detective Flynn shot you?"

He looked up again and tried to focus. "What?"

"I'm Vicky Rose. I'm a reporter," she explained. "I need to know, were you unarmed?"

Vicky quickly realized that he was too drugged-up to answer any questions. Something else she should have anticipated. This whole thing had been a bust. And it was about to go downhill from there.

"Yep, there she is. Just like you said," she heard a Nurse exclaim from the doorway. Vicky looked up to see Nurse Olivia, arms crossed and brow furrowed.

To one side of her was the Police Officer, shaking his head with a stern expression. And on the other side was Denny. With that same sheepish look on his face that he always had.

Holding a damn bouquet of flowers.

WORTHINGTON needed a moment to himself. He had no idea why Bridget's words had suddenly affected him. Perhaps it was because it was the very question he'd asked himself so many times these past fifteen years. And it was one for which he had no ready answer.

He quickly dismissed the girls and sent them back to their duties. He'd thought about retreating to his quarters, but it was too close to both the kitchen and the laundry. He needed a place of assured solitude.

He took the elevator up to the third floor, which was largely unused. This was where the staff had been housed back when they had other live-in servants besides him. From there he opened a tiny door and took a narrow staircase up to the attic. In times of sorrow, this was where he preferred to retreat with his memories.

And where they had stored the Gregors' old clothes,

particularly Sarah's. Brent had kept a few of his father's things downstairs, but had no ready use for his mother's. Worthington had suggested that they donate them, but Brent refused to give them up. He wanted to keep every single dress.

Except one.

So they had finished off a portion of the attic had it converted into a salon of sorts, complete with racks for her many dresses, shelves for her hats and shoes, and drawers for her jewelry. It looked like a showplace for a time long past.

In their college years, Brent and Abbie had retreated up there on more than one occasion. Abbie had loved to try on Mrs. Gregor's gowns. She'd always admired her elegance and sense of style. And Brent loved to watch her model them.

Worthington had been worried that one of them might get torn, but he needn't have. Abbie was always careful to take the utmost care and put each garment back exactly how she had found it.

Such happier times, he thought. Then he wondered if such happiness would ever return to this house again.

With thoughts both bitter and sweet weighing upon his heart, he perused the racks. For every article, there was a memory. Usually one that made him smile fondly.

He'd expected them to smell musty, but was surprised that they did not. After closer inspection, he noticed that some had been freshly laundered.

Curious, he thought.

He took a quick inventory. Nothing seemed out of place, however. All was present and accounted for. Even the jewelry.

Perhaps Mrs. Poole had been keeping the items cared for. He would have to ask her about it when she returned.

DENNY tried repeatedly to apologize, all the way back to Vicky's hospital room and even more after they'd arrived. It was all to no avail. Vicky remained coldly silent.

As a final gesture of his heartfelt sincerity, he handed her the bouquet of flowers. But she just threw them back at his head, sending the assorted buds scattering in all directions. That was when she finally broke her silence.

"That was my best opportunity! And you ruined it!"

"I'm sorry," he apologized yet again, "but the Doctor said you need to rest. I was just trying to help."

Vicky seethed in her fury. It was a good thing they were in a hospital, she thought. Because Denny was seconds away from needing medical attention.

"You're not my husband, Denny," she fumed. "You don't own me. Not you. Not Frank. Not my father. Nobody!"

It didn't take a genius to realize he'd struck a major nerve. "I was just trying to help," he whimpered.

But Vicky wasn't finished. "And if you want to be my... boyfriend any longer, you need to realize, I make my own decisions. So just back off or get the hell out!"

"I'm sorry," was all he could manage in response.

Denny couldn't help but notice the pause before she said "boyfriend." That had stung the hardest. He'd already been on shaky ground.

And somehow, he'd just made it worse.

CHAPTER FOURTEEN

WORTHINGTON met with Mrs. Poole first thing Monday morning. The question of Mrs. Gregor's dresses had nagged at him all night. And after all the circumstances of the last several days, he was anxious to put the matter to rest.

One less thing on his mind.

He went straight down to the servant's kitchen and found her eating breakfast. Fortunately, the other maids were already about their duties. And Mr. Coleman was off on his weekly trip to the market.

The question had so nagged at him, that he completely brushed over his comments regarding the laundry inspection.

"Oh yes," she readily admitted. "We clean them every year or so. Don't want nothing happening to those."

That seemed to answer it then. Worthington felt an immediate sense of relief. As a long-standing employee himself, he couldn't help but appreciate her dedication.

"They're about due for another cleaning I'd say," she offered.

"Very good. Thank you, Mrs. Poole."

Then she added, "That Mrs. Gregor, she was such a lovely woman. I still miss her so."

Worthington felt the emotion get the better of him. "As do we all, Ma'am. As do we all."

VICKY waited with Frank outside the front of the hospital while Betty went to retrieve the car. True to form, she told the discharge nurse she didn't need a wheelchair and walked out on her own. Which probably hadn't been the best idea.

She didn't notice Frank's anger and disappointment until the awkward silence made it impossible to miss. "I'm taking you off the crime beat until further notice," he informed her.

"What?" she reacted with surprise. "Please tell me you're not serious."

"I've got half a mind to ground you completely," he grumbled. "I'm doing this for your own good. Doctor's orders."

She fumed under her breath. Fortunately she managed to hold her tongue, because every response that immediately came to mind would have likely gotten her fired.

He sounded just like Denny. *That snitch*, she thought. *This was all his fault.*

Then a formidable thought struck her. "You're not sending me back to City Hall, are you?"

"John Brown-it, Red, you sound like Lyons." If only he had stopped there. But she wasn't about to get off that easy. "You can help Leonore on the Society page."

"What the hell, Frank?" she barked. "That's even worse! You know Leonore *hates* me."

"Well, maybe next time you'll listen."

MRS. POOLE, Mollie, and Bridget worked to pull the latest load of bed sheets and table cloths from the drying rack and get them folded. The racks were in a large cabinet with vertical drawers. Each drawer was fitted with metal bars to hang the linens. After the drawers were slid back into the cabinet, heat was pumped through. It was so much quicker and easier than line drying like they did in their own homes.

An explosion of gunfire echoed down the hall.

The women screamed and instinctively dropped to the floor.

Once they'd gotten their wits about them, they stood back up. For Mrs. Poole, it took a little longer than the younger girls.

Moments later, more shots rang out. Only then, it was expected.

"Sounds like Master Gregor's done finally come out of his room," Mollie remarked.

"Just wish we'd known beforehand," Mrs. Poole added. "My heart can't take surprises like that."

BRENT reloaded his .45 pistol. He'd spent close to three days holed up in his room stewing in anger and disappointment. Having been lost in his thoughts for that length of time had only made matters worse.

A trip downstairs to the indoor shooting range was the perfect antidote. It wasn't a cure for his ills, of course. But it certainly made him feel better.

His father had installed the range many years earlier. It was essentially a long, narrow concrete bunker built into the basement, next to the laundry. Brent had many fond memories watching his father and grandfather practice on the rotating tin targets. Many still bore the dents.

Brent steadied himself in his chair and unloaded another clip in rapid succession. Over the years of using the range for sport and (more typically) to let off steam, he'd managed to become a rather good shot.

He blasted one of the tiny ducks clear off the armature. He'd have to get Mr. Donaldson to fix it.

True to his nature, he'd spent those last three days analyzing every choice. Every argument. And every mistake. He'd played an endless series of "what ifs?"

What if he hadn't played that insipid game? What if Amrish hadn't rescued him from that mountain? What if the surgery had worked? What if he'd gone and apologized to Abbie before she flew back to Emerson?

Those thoughts eventually led him further back. Back to the ultimate *what if* question. *What if he had never been shot?*

That's where it all began. If Ned Vogel hadn't come into their house that night, nearly his entire life would have been different.

And it was all because of Big Jack.

Big Jack was the root cause of all the pain in his life. The loss of his parents. His ability to walk. And ultimately the loss of Abbie.

His father had tried to take Big Jack down. He'd had the right idea. But he'd gone about it the wrong way.

That was increasingly clear.

There was only one way to deal with men like Big Jack. The same way he'd taken taken over the North Side.

You cut the head off the beast.

Brent unloaded another clip. With his powers, he could easily kill him. He'd get his revenge, and the city would declare him a hero.

Certainly a bigger hero than those two cops in that farce of an awards ceremony.

As he reloaded, a thought occurred to him. His powers. Surely he'd be just as good a shot standing on his feet. Why wouldn't he?

Because Ned Vogel had easily gotten the better of him that night at the Asylum. Yes, he had these abilities, but he hadn't yet learned how to use them. He was too untrained.

Brent extended a hand towards the door. It easily locked. He knew no one would bother him while he was doing target practice. But it was best to be sure.

Then he closed his eyes and gripped the arm rests of his wheelchair. The ornate ring on his finger glowed brightly and the long, narrow room grew suddenly cold.

He moved his feet to the floor and stood up. Somehow he'd grown stronger than before. Even from just a few days earlier with Abbie.

He picked up his pistol and looked down range. It felt so strange to hold it while he was standing.

He suddenly felt less sure of himself.

He tried to remember how he'd seen his father and grandfather do it. One foot forward, one foot back. For some reason, it didn't feel right. But then again, how could it?

He wondered if he should call for Worthington. But then he just as quickly dismissed the idea. Worthington was no marksman.

That would be Mr. Donaldson. They'd shared the range on more than one occasion. He'd even let Mr. Donaldson and the guards use it themselves.

But inviting Mr. Donaldson would involve a great deal of explaining. So he just as quickly dismissed that idea as well.

Brent made his best guess on the proper stance. He was unprepared for just how foreign it felt.

He aimed at the target. A rotating rabbit.

He pulled the trigger.

Next thing he knew, he was sprawled on the floor. And he'd completely missed the rabbit.

This would require far more practice.

VITO SPATS took off his bowler hat and still had to duck as he stepped down through the tiny doorway into the opium den. Right behind him was Willie and Fingers.

The basement room was filled with cots and pillows. Nearly every one occupied by a man smoking an opium pipe, or already in a state of unconsciousness, hallucinating from the sweet aroma.

The den was run by an old Chinese man who sat silently in a corner. A handful of young Chinese women assisted him, and for the right price would provide more pleasures than what was supplied by the opium alone.

Spats quickly scanned the dark, candle-lit room for an Irishman with white hair. According to his sources, Whitey O'Leary had been known to visit this particular location. But it was too dark to see very far. And he wasn't sure how reliable the information was anyway. His best bet was to just make it known for whom he was searching.

Spats approached the proprietor. He had no idea if the old man spoke any English. Or Italian for that matter. So he assumed neither.

Spats pointed to his own hair and said, "Báisè," which he'd been told was the Chinese word for "white." Then he pointed towards the scattered cots.

The old Chinaman just stared back, unblinking. Either he didn't understand or just didn't care to. More than likely he was laughing on the inside at this large, Italian man's pitiful attempt at his language. But he did a good job of hiding it.

The Chinese were very good at keeping secrets.

IT WAS late in the afternoon when Vicky stepped into the front hallway of Mrs. Hershey's Boarding House for Women. She turned and waved to Frank, who waited in his car, to let him know that she was safely inside. It had been a quiet ride home. Even with Betty in the car with them, the tension alone was deafening.

She could feel yet another headache returning. All she wanted to do was get her mail, pop a dose of her new medication, and go to bed. She had an even bigger headache to face in the morning.

She had just plucked her mailbox key from her purse when, as usual, Mrs. Hershey poked her head outside her first floor doorway to see who had arrived. The older woman made a point of keeping track of all of her boarders and strictly enforced the curfew. Speaking of headaches.

"Oh, you've returned," Mrs. Hershey remarked with pleasant surprise as she handed her a note. "You had a telephone message from your sister. She called more than once, actually. Said it was important that you call her back right away."

"Oh, thank you," Vicky said as she took the note and gave it a quick glance. More than likely, Father had probably taken yet another turn for the worse. Nothing new there.

She glanced down at her watch. It was almost too late to call back. But more importantly, it wasn't anything she was prepared to deal with just then. But still...

"I assume it had to do with you being in the hospital," Mrs. Hershey added with a hint of embarrassment. "Of course, I didn't know that when she called. Otherwise, I would have said something. Don't want her to think I was uncaring. I do hope it's nothing serious."

That last part took Vicky off guard. "Wait, how did you know I was in the hospital?"

"Oh, your gentleman caller told me," she replied. "Yesterday evening, when he came to pick up your mail. Normally, I would never have let him do such a thing. But when he explained that you were in the hospital, well, I just thought it was quite chivalrous, you know."

Vicky angrily stuck her key into the lock and opened the tiny metal door. Sure enough, it was empty.

She inhaled sharply and grimaced in frustration. *That Denny!*

CHAPTER FIFTEEN

DETECTIVE FLYNN walked into the precinct to thunderous applause. Both from his fellow officers and the handful of reporters who'd "gotten wind" of his return to work. He was back in his dress uniform with his arm in a crisp, white sling. It was like he'd just stepped off the stage back at Harrison Park.

After getting bathed in flashbulbs, Lyons, Hecht, Gelbart, and the other newshounds crowded around him with the usual barrage of fawning questions. Flynn was happy that the skirt was nowhere to be seen. He could only assume she'd been fired, and rightfully so.

"How's it feel to be back, Lieutenant?" Charlie asked.

"Doc told me not to come back so soon," he boasted, "but it's gonna take more than a bullet to keep me off the job!"

The reporters all erupted in laughter and showered him in another barrage of flashbulbs.

Shayne walked in just in time so see this latest edition of the ongoing circus. And he just as quickly stepped right back out before anyone saw him.

VICKY took a deep breath, swallowed her pride, and steeled her nerves. Reporting in to work with Leonore was the last thing she wanted to face.

Hopefully, she thought, Leonore wouldn't even be there. She'd just gotten back from Los Angeles and chances were pretty good that the society maven would come in late.

No such luck. As soon as she rounded the corner, she

saw her dark-haired nemesis, feet propped up on her desk, reading the morning edition.

In a building terribly short on space, Leonore had somehow managed to wrangle her own office. Certainly through a combination of feminine charm and implied family connections. She was never shy about throwing out her famous last name. Despite only being a distant cousin.

"Good morning!" Leonore chirped sarcastically just as soon as Vicky darkened her door. Her tone was decidedly less friendly and more *I look forward to torturing you.*

"Good morning," Vicky replied. She started to say something else, but then changed her mind. *The less said the better*, she thought.

Still, nothing would keep Leonore from relishing the moment. "So, ready for your first assignment?"

She didn't wait for Vicky to answer. Which was just as well, because she would have been waiting a long time. "I realize this isn't the *hard-hitting journalism* you're used to, but there's a function to-night in Lakeview Heights. Everyone who's everyone will be there."

Leonore knew just where it would hurt the most.

Vicky gritted her teeth. This was already more than she had bargained for. Hobnobbing with the local blue bloods and writing gossip pieces about their small talk was decidedly not her idea of journalism.

But she was also smart enough to know that this wasn't Leonore's only game. Clearly she had an ulterior motive. This was just a reverse bait and switch to get what she really wanted.

"Look," Vicky protested. "Can't I just write some copy for you? I can do all the *dot dot dot* and *a little bird told me*, the whole nine yards. No one will know the difference."

"I'm glad you *appreciate* the subtleties of my writing style," Leonore feigned a smile. "But I need you to chat up Louisa Crocetti."

"The Mobster's daughter?" Vicky asked.

"Exactly," Leonore chirped. "Should be right up your alley. You two practically run in the same circles."

Vicky just shook her head and gritted her teeth some more. She was determined not to let Leonore get to her.

But she wasn't doing a very good job of it. "I can't go to something like that. I simply don't have a dress for it."

"Knew you'd say that," Leonore chirped right back. "Run down to Vivian's. She'll find you something. Charge it to the paper, so nothing too expensive. But nothing that will embarrass me, either."

Vicky just stood there and stewed. This was not helping her headaches in the least. She was going to kill Frank.

"Okay, Leonore. We're both professionals here." Vicky figured a little flattery wouldn't hurt. But she also knew that Leonore wouldn't buy it. "Let's just cut the malarkey. What is it you really want?"

"Okay, you want to make a deal?" Leonore replied. "Here it is. A little bird told me that a certain eligible bachelor went to California to profess his undying love to the one that got away. Only to find out that she'd just gotten married. You get any kind of statement on the record, even a denial, and I'll tell Frank whatever you want to get you back on the crime beat."

Vicky almost had to take a step back on that one. "I can't," she said emphatically. "I won't."

"Oh, that's so sad. And personal." Leonore was more than surprised. "So, why not?"

"Because, I can't do that to him," Vicky stated. "And besides, I barely know him."

"Well then, you'd better get down to Vivian's," Leonore smiled. "Run along, now. She's expecting you."

CHAPTER SIXTEEN

KID YELLOW woke up groggily to a splash of cold water in his face. His eyes were swollen, his head bleeding, and his arms and whole body ached beyond belief.

He'd been dangling by his arms all night, his wrists shackled and hanging from a chain thrown over a girder overhead. They'd carried him to a warehouse up by the river where Tommy and Fingers had taken turns pounding on him all night. As much as he wanted to die, he was amazed he was still alive.

They hadn't even asked him anything for the first few hours. Then it was just one question over and over. Only he didn't know the answer. No matter how hard they beat on him.

Willie grabbed him by the hair and lifted his head up. "Wake up, sleepy head! Got somebody here wants to talk to you."

Willie let go and let his head drop back down. Yellow didn't even have to see the man's gleaming white spats to know who it was. He knew he'd show up sooner or later. And since Spats no longer did this sort of work himself, it had been much, much later.

Now that Big Jack's underboss had arrived, it could only mean that the worst was still to come.

"I don't know nothing, I swear," Yellow gurgled, hoping death would come soon. He knew Spats' reputation. He'd heard the stories about previous victims.

"Now you hang on just a minute," Willie scolded. "Spats

ain't even asked you nothing yet."

Yellow wondered for just a second if maybe Spats was going to ask him something different. But then he didn't. "I just need you to tell me, where can I find Whitey O'Leary?"

"I don't know!" Yellow weeped for what seemed like the hundredth time. "I swear! I don't know!"

Spats put his walking stick under Yellow's chin and lifted his head. Yellow could barely see the Italian mobster's wax-tipped moustache through his blood-soaked eyes.

"Do you want to die without any more pain?" Spats asked. Yellow nodded in affirmation.

"Then just tell me where I can find Whitey O'Leary."

"I don't know," Yellow sobbed. "I swear on my mother's life, I tell you. They don't tell me nothing!"

Willie leaned over to Spats and whispered, "You know, I'm thinking maybe he's telling the truth. He really don't know nothing."

Spats replied, "Of course, he don't. Nails ain't that stupid. No, we gotta make Kid Yellow an example here. So, the next guy we grab, he'll be ready to talk."

Willie nodded in agreement. "Okay, I got you."

"Good," Spats replied. "Now get the hammer."

SHAYNE stepped into Flynn's office and closed the door. He looked anxiously through the large glass windows. The cramped room faced the bullpen and even with the door shut, offered little privacy. Flynn glanced up from his paperwork, attempting to manage it with just one hand. "Something on your mind, Bob?"

"Yeah," Shayne replied nervously. He quickly sat down and leaned across Flynn's desk. "We gotta talk."

Flynn looked up to make sure no one was watching. Or listening. "I'm not sure I've got time for this, Bob. I'm a busy man. You'll know what it's like now that you've been promoted."

That whole thought just riled Shayne even more. He knew he deserved it, but he sure as hell didn't like the way it'd happened. Or how they'd made a monkey of him in front of the entire city.

"I just don't like how this whole situation is shaking out,"

Shayne grumbled.

"Don't act all surprised, Bob," Flynn chastised him. "You know how things work in this town. You've gotten your share of the retirement fund."

"Yeah, I do," Shayne retorted. "I know when to keep my mouth shut. Only now I got Willie Potatoes parked outside my house. Watching my wife do laundry while my kid plays in the back yard!"

"Listen," Flynn whispered forcefully. "Don't go soft on me! I took a bullet!"

"Yeah, well I did, too!" Shayne snapped back. "Only somebody *else* pulled the trigger."

Flynn jumped to his feet, knocking his chair back against the wall. The men in the bullpen quickly turned to look. Wondering what the commotion was all about.

Flynn reached for his chair, casually pulled it back to his desk. He fumed to himself and collected his thoughts. Waited for the men to go back to their business.

"You just keep your mouth shut and you'll be a hero for the rest of your life, you got me?" Flynn reminded him. "Unless you want your family to end up on the street."

"You don't got to worry about me," Shayne told him. Then he took the wad cash Willie had given him and threw it on Flynn's desk.

"Here's your thirty pieces of silver."

Flynn instinctively scooped it up. It disappeared so fast, it was like it had never been there.

DENNY lit up the moment he saw Vicky breeze into the morgue. His expression dropped just as quickly when he saw the look in her eyes. Clearly, the feeling wasn't mutual. *Was it something else he'd done?* he wondered. Or because she was working for Leonore? Or both?

"So how's your first day back at work?" he stammered.

"Leonore's got me going to this shindig to-morrow night for all the local blue bloods," she grumbled. "Spent the whole afternoon at a dress shop getting poked and prodded while they pointed out every where I could stand to lose a smidge."

Denny didn't know what to say. He couldn't imagine

anyone thinking she was anything less than perfect.

She let out a huff of frustration and immediately switched topics. "So, you got my mail?"

"Of course!" he answered with a chivalrous grin. "I've got it right here." And that's when he realized it wasn't just Leonore.

"You really didn't have to do that," she snapped as she plucked the handful of letters from his hand. "I can get my own mail, thank you."

Denny stumbled all over himself trying to apologize. She'd only just agreed to this courtship. And he surely didn't want it to end so quickly.

"I'm sorry," he mumbled. "About this. About the hospital. Everything."

He hoped that if he just kept talking, she wouldn't walk out. At least not right away. "I was just trying to help out, that's all. Please, you've got to understand. I didn't mean anything by it. I swear."

She closed her eyes for a moment and gathered her thoughts. Then after taking a deep inhale, she spelled it all out for him.

"Denny, there's something you need to understand about me. I make my own decisions. Sometimes good, sometimes bad. But they're mine. I don't need you, or Frank, or my father, or anyone else to look out for me. And if you can't abide by that, then there's no point in seeing each other anymore."

He looked back at her like a whipped puppy. "I was just trying to help, is all."

She could have sworn she saw his lower lip quiver.

DETECTIVE SHAYNE wormed his way into the dark, junk-filled alley until he finally reached the crime scene. A young Beat Cop paced nervously about, trying desperately not to look at the victim. He was surprised to find that *Daily Crusader* reporter Chester Lyons was already on the scene. But then again, he shouldn't have been.

"Who tipped you off, Lyons?" Shayne grumbled.

"Got my ear to the ground, what can I say?" Lyons smirked.

The young Beat Cop quickly looked away. Couldn't have been on the force for more than a year, but he already knew the drill. Of course, it would take him a lot longer before he could stomach crime scenes like this one.

Sprawled on the brick pavement in a pool of blood was the body, all twisted and broken, arms and legs going off in unnatural directions. And with his eyes still wide open, it was a hell of a sight to see. It would take a lot of alcohol to forget it, Shayne thought. A lot more than usual.

"Any idea who he is?" the Beat Cop asked as he struggled to light a cigarette.

"Yeah," Lyons told him. "Name's Arvid Newman. But they call him Kid Yellow."

Pretty low-level guy to end up like this, Shayne thought. Yellow never hurt a soul. He was just an errand boy. Wasn't too bright. Didn't know a thing. Couldn't even tell you the time of day.

"Looks like he drank himself to death," Lyons commented sarcastically. "Maybe took a walk off the roof."

"Yeah," Shayne added. "Looks like he beat the ever living hell out of himself, too."

BRENT closed his eyes and took a deep breath. His feet were planted firmly on the ground. His stance was perfect. His grip was solid. The room was cold.

He exhaled slowly and opened his eyes. He had a clear view of the target.

He stared down the barrel and took aim.

He squeezed the trigger.

He unloaded the entire clip on a rabbit as it rotated into sight.

A second later, the rabbit was gone. Only the bare stub of an armature completed its rotation.

Brent felt good. For the first time in days, in fact.

Suddenly, it all made sense. How he could correct all the wrongs that had been committed against so many. How he would use his newfound abilities to bring down Big Jack. No one would ever suspect it was him. It was the perfect disguise.

He would truly *bring justice to those who have none.*

Most especially, himself.

He'd spent the better part of a day down in the range. He'd gotten Worthington to retrieve a book on marksmanship and exhausted most of his supply of ammunition. He felt himself grow even stronger.

Only one question remained.

He'd never taken a man's life before, of course. This would be a lot different than rotating ducks made of tin.

There was every possibility that he'd have to shoot his target close up.

When the moment came, could he do it? Could he pull the trigger?

All he had to do was think about that night. Seeing with his own young eyes what had happened to his father. To his mother.

To him.

CHAPTER SEVENTEEN

Five Years Prior.

BRENT and Abbie had only been back at Emerson University for just over a month when he received a summons to report to the administration building. At once. So he wheeled himself down the wood-floored hallway to President Nolan's office. Brent had previously met the administrator upon arrival and many times since. Nolan was both eager to have the young Mr. Gregor as a student and was more than willing to accommodate his specific needs.

Naturally, he wondered if he was being reprimanded for some unknown infraction. But he'd always been a model student and, considering his handicap, was given a bit more leeway than the other students. Which came in handy for Abbie's frequent curfew violations.

He was just about to knock on the outer office door when Mrs. Keating stepped out to greet him. She was a dumpy, middle-aged spinster who was married to the university.

"Ah, young Mr. Gregor, if you'd..." she paused, searching for words other than her usual phrase *take a seat*, "wait out here for just a moment. President Nolan will be with you shortly."

Then she quickly ducked right back inside and closed the door. He heard a muffled "Mr. Gregor is here."

President Nolan then asked about *her*, but Brent was unable to make out anything beyond that.

Curfew violations, he thought. That had to be it.

His suspicions seemed proven correct when he heard approaching footsteps coming from down the wooden floors of the hallway. He looked up to see Abbie fasten the top button of her blouse, straighten her skirt, and do her utmost to look innocent and respectful. The picture perfect Emerson student.

Abbie looked just as anxious as she sat down on the bench next to him. "Any idea what this is about?" she asked.

"Curfew," Brent replied succinctly.

"Think Fruehauf finally ratted us out?"

Brent snickered uncontrollably. Abbie chuckled back with surprise. "What's so humorous?"

"You sound like a Cagney movie," he explained. "Just need a cigarette dangling from your lip."

She smiled back defiantly, "Well, at least we have something to laugh about before they kick us out."

He noticed she never spoke like that before she started flying.

"Spending too much time with those pilot friends of yours," Brent remarked. His jealous streak at last showing through.

Before they had time to debate either of those statements, the door swung open and Mrs. Keating beckoned them in. "Mr. Gregor, President Nolan is ready to see you now," she instructed. "And Miss Wentworth, if you would join me in my office."

Abbie helped wheel him inside the outer office and then through the doorway on the left into President Nolan's private chambers. She parked him right in front of Nolan's desk. The Headmaster looked stern but anxious. He didn't say a word to her. Clearly this was going to be bad news.

"Thank you, Miss Wentworth," Mrs. Keating said matter-of-factly from behind. Abbie gave Brent one more confused look before she walked out and Mrs. Keating closed the door.

And that's how Brent found out that his mother had died.

To spare him from immediately having to share the news himself, Mrs. Keating had graciously agreed to tell Abbie at the same time. Due to the nature of their relationship and out of deference to his *particular circumstances*, she was also given leave to accompany him home for the funeral.

President Nolan praised him for his stoicism upon hearing the news. But the truth of the matter was, he'd already lost his mother long ago and had no idea how to react.

He found Abbie outside waiting for him.

"I'm just so sorry, Brent," she told him tearfully, then bent down and kissed him.

"So am I," he told her. "So am I."

BRENT and Abbie booked first class accommodations on the evening train home, for arrival in Terminal City the next morning. It actually took a bit of convincing for Worthington to allow them to return home on their own. Decorum dictated that he should escort the two back, despite the fact that they'd already made the train ride on their own several times. Decorum also dictated two separate cabins, even though one went largely unused.

In the end, practicality was the deciding factor. There simply wasn't enough time for Worthington to make the trip in Smithson & Gregor's private rail car, escort them home, and still arrive for the funeral service in a timely manner.

After his promise to never see his mother again, Brent wondered if that might apply to her funeral as well. Abbie surprised him by agreeing to go to the service.

She'd felt a sudden rush of guilt for asking him to make such a vow. And even worse when he asked if she was willing to join him.

She assured him that she would never leave his side.

BRENT and Abbie found a small contingent of people waiting on the platform at Union Station for their arrival. In addition to Worthington, of course, there was Mr. Coleman, and the Wentworth family chauffeur, Mr. Peterson.

But the real surprise was Abbie's older brother, Billy, looking very dashing in his pinstriped suit. He'd promised their parents to look after his younger sister, and he was there to do just that.

"Billy!" Abbie exclaimed, "what on earth?"

"Well, the office is nearby," Billy offered, "so I thought, what better way to welcome you home?"

As Worthington directed the porters to set up the ramp for Brent to disembark, Abbie bounded off the train and gave her brother a heartfelt embrace. She also pulled down her hair to hide the faint scar on her cheek.

Billy knew, of course, that she and Brent had become romantically involved. But he was uneasy about actually seeing them together. Despite being longtime neighbors, he honestly didn't know Brent very well. This was as much due to their age difference as it was to Brent's handicap.

He and their parents had imagined a specific life for Abbie. And it didn't involve being a caretaker for the infirm. Even if he did come from a good family. Of course, it didn't involve her becoming a pilot, either.

As surprised as Abbie was to see Billy, she was also wary. She suspected an ulterior motive. And was soon proven correct.

"Actually, Sis," he suggested, "I've got plenty of room in the apartment. Thought you might want to stay downtown while you're home. Give us some time to catch up."

Abbie knew that meant he'd shooed off his girlfriend for a few days. The younger Wentworth wasn't the only one to present an illusion of decorum. "Maybe one night," Abbie told him. "But Brent really needs me right now. And I really want to be there for him."

Abbie stayed at the Wentworth Mansion the entire time she was home. At least that's the way it appeared.

THE GROUP of mourners at Sarah Gregor's funeral was small but influential. Most were friends, staff, and acquaintances. Brent was glad that despite his sheltered upbringing, he knew almost everyone there. And for the few names he couldn't remember, Abbie was quick to whisper in his ear.

As he sat on the front row with both her and Worthington at his side, he couldn't help but be reminded of the chilly morning ten years earlier when his father was buried: the large granite monument that towered behind the casket.

The name GREGOR was chiseled in grand letters across the top. To the left read "THOMAS, Loving Father, Devoted Son." His dates of birth and death inscribed below.

For these past ten years the right side had been blank. Its cold, stone surface waiting patiently for Sarah to die.

Right next to it was another towering, half-inscribed tombstone, about which Brent was equally troubled. This one bore the name of his grandmother. Katherine Dawson Gregor had passed away twelve years prior, stricken with tuberculosis. Afterwards, a broken-hearted Nate Gregor turned his back on his business and family (young Brent included) and soon married a beautiful, young violinist.

Following the service, which was beautifully delivered by Father Ryan, the mourners all went over to Brent to pay their respects.

First in line was "Uncle Dick" Smithson and Aunt Amelia. With them were Dick Jr. and his wife, Alice, and the rest of the Smithson dynasty. Even Dick Jr's little daughter, Elsie. As Grandpa Nate's business partner and co-founder of Smithson & Gregor, the Smithsons were the closest Brent had to an actual family.

Brent's eyes lit up at the sight of Nanny Miriam, who came with Mr. Coleman, Mrs. Poole, and the other members of the staff. He promised to have her over again under better circumstances.

Billy was there, too, of course. He shook Brent's hand and offered his condolences, but said little else. Abbie had already explained why.

As much as he cared for Dr. Wellman and his wife, Muriel, they were yet another reminder of past tragedy. The Wellmans had previously lived nearby and had rushed to the Gregors aid that fateful Halloween.

Abbie knew to introduce his mother's friends, whom he vaguely recognized but had no idea who they were. Both told him how kind and gentle she was. That was the woman he wanted so desperately to remember.

Most surprising of all was the presence of Julius Kennelly, who came with his beautiful young wife, Marguerite. Sadly, he seemed intoxicated and suggested that Abbie visit him afterwards. She politely declined, though what she really wanted to do was far less ladylike.

District Attorney Doc Milford was the only one there from City Hall. He shook Brent's hand and offered simply, "The Mayor sends his regrets."

Milford shifted uncomfortably and was about to dash off before he stopped to add, "Your father was a fine man." Brent found it odd that Doc Milford said nothing about his mother. But perhaps, he reasoned, the flamboyant D.A. didn't really know her that well.

Among the wreaths was one from Sarah's sole remaining relative, her elderly Aunt Charlotte who deeply regretted that she couldn't make the trip. At 91 years old, she lived alone in a 5th Avenue Manhattan apartment. She'd inherited her wealth from her father who'd built his fortune in copper mining. She took Sarah in and raised her after the girl's missionary parents had died in Egypt.

She'd never failed to send Brent a crisp ten dollar bill on his birthday, even in his teenage years. A few weeks after they'd returned to Emerson, Brent and Abbie made a point of taking the train down to Manhattan one weekend for a visit. She was still sharp as ever and regaled them with wonderful stories about his mother's childhood and her courtship with his father. It was the closest Brent had ever felt to his own family. And a clear reminder that he was largely an orphan.

Much to Brent's disappointment, Grandpa Nate and his young family remained in Paris. Brent had hoped that they might board a ship and return home. It was impossible for them to make it in time for the funeral, he knew. But he hadn't seen his grandfather in years. And after Grandpa Nate missing his own son's funeral due to a quirk of fate, Brent was sure he'd want to return.

Instead they merely sent flowers and their condolences via telegram. And not much else.

CHAPTER EIGHTEEN

VICKY cautiously peered around the corner into the City Room. As she'd hoped, Frank was still out having a late lunch at the Cosmic Diner. On Wednesday they served mashed potatoes, so she knew he'd return later than usual. She was right.

Luckily, Lyons has just gotten back from lunch himself. Shockingly enough. Just the man she wanted to see. "What're you doing in here, Kid?" he asked as she snuck quietly in. "Aren't you supposed to be sharpening pencils for Leonore?"

"Just wanted to ask you about the Kid Yellow murder," she answered quietly.

Lyons just brushed her off. "Who says it was murder?"

"Come on, Lyons," she chastised him. "You're not talking to some wet-behind-the-ears pencil pusher."

"Oh?" he retorted.

With Frank possibly due back any minute, she didn't have time to argue. "So, what's the word on the street? You think Big Jack was behind it?"

"Listen Kid," Lyons sighed. "Frank says you're grounded and that's A-OK with me. So why don't you run on back to Leonore and pick out wallpaper or whatever you gals do. Leave the real reporting to us men."

Vicky inhaled sharply. Should have known he wasn't about to help her. She had so many things she wanted to say to him, but was in no position to say them.

She was just about to leave when Perry Phillips thrust

another stack of messages into her hand. "That Spider fellow keeps calling. And your sister called, too. She said it was urgent."

It probably was, she thought. But nothing she had time to deal with just then.

Worse still, she felt another headache coming on.

WILLIE POTATOES stood up from his chair in the stark interrogation room as Shayne barreled in. Willie'd been sitting there a good two hours already without a peep from anyone. Not that he was surprised, mind you.

"Hey, lookit, it's the hero Copper!" Willie remarked cheerfully. "Can I get your autograph?"

Shayne gripped Willie's injured shoulder and shoved him back in his seat. Willie ignored the pain and just smirked in response.

Both men knew the score. Shayne's job was to harass and intimidate Willie in the hopes that he'd give up some piece of information. Or at least make Big Jack think he had. And at 6 foot 2 with a physique forged in the United States Marines, Shayne could be very intimidating indeed.

But Willie wasn't like the usual street punks who sat in that chair. He knew that if he could get in Shayne's head, he could throw the bull off his game. And if he had to take a beating, well, he'd already had worse than anything this copper could dish out. Even with a bum shoulder.

Shayne paced around him like a lion considering its prey. Then he took off his jacket and rolled up his sleeves. This was his first case as a detective. And even though he didn't like how he'd gotten there, he was still determined to make a good show of it. At least prove he deserved it.

"What can you tell me about the Kid Yellow murder?" Shayne grumbled. There was little doubt who was behind it. The only real questions were who actually did the deed and whether or not the police could prove it.

"Only what I read in the papers," Willie smirked. "Heard he got ripped and took a walk off a roof."

With his arm still in a sling, Willie had a pretty decent alibi. But as Spats' right-hand man, chances were he knew exactly who was responsible.

Shayne grabbed him by the shoulder with one of his giant mitts and squeezed down hard like a vice. Willie gave a little wince, but he never lost his smile. "How's that arm feeling, Willie?" Shayne sneered.

"Tripped on the sidewalk, what can I say?" Willie sang back.

"Not how I heard it," Shayne grumbled.

Willie just rolled his eyes. "Oh yeah?"

Shayne gripped his shoulder even tighter and leaned in close. "I heard you were at the Belmont a few weeks back. Heard you took a bullet."

"Yeah, well if I did," Willie retorted with a laugh, "at least I got mine legit."

That was all it took. Shayne angrily knocked the table over and grabbed a still-smiling Willie by the collar. "What do you know?" Shayne demanded angrily.

"What's the matter, *Detective*?" Willie chuckled. "Looks like I ain't the only one with a sore spot, huh?"

VICKY stormed into the Cosmic and shoved herself into the booth across from Frank. Clearly, this was not a social call. "No need to hurry, Red," he told her. "They've got plenty of mashed potatoes. Really good this week, too."

Vicky skipped the pleasantries and went straight to brass tacks. "Leonore's got me going to this society function to-night. A bunch of blue bloods drinking champaign and dressing to the nines."

"So, what's your point?" Frank asked.

"My point is that I should be going to the opening of The Four Diamonds instead," she complained. "That's more my style."

"So, you want to skip one social event just so you can go to another?" he asked, feigning puzzlement.

"Don't play dumb with me, Frank," she barked. "You know as well as I do, if the North Siders want to attack Big Jack, that's the perfect place to do it!"

"Yeah, well," he replied, "that's just not the sort of thing we cover in the Society page. If Leonore needs you to go to that function, then that's where you go."

Vicky exhaled sharply. "At least tell me who you're

sending."

"Perry," he stated.

"Seriously? Can't you at least send Lyons? He's a jerk, but at least he's better than Perry."

"I've got Lyons working another story," Frank explained.

"The Kid Yellow murder?" she asked.

"None of your business, Red," he replied calmly.

Of course she already knew about that, he thought. Nothing got by this gal. That's why she was such a good reporter. Which made it all that much harder to steer her away.

"You realize, you're killing me, Frank," Vicky complained. "Let me cover this one and *then* you can ground me."

"*You* realize, I'm doing this to save your life," he replied. "How're the headaches?"

Vicky didn't respond. She just looked away, angrily.

"Just what I thought," he told her. "Have fun at the party. And get over to the hair dresser before they close."

"Something tells me you're enjoying this," she snapped back.

BRENT loaded another clip at the table in his room. He'd brought up every box of ammunition he had left. Even with the ability to disappear into the shadows, he knew he'd be going up against an army with pistols and more. He had to be prepared.

Worthington, of course, had a differing opinion. "Sir, I do beg you to reconsider this course of action. Might I remind you that all did not go well at the Asylum. And that was but a short time ago."

"Why be given these abilities if I can't use them for good?" Brent challenged.

Worthington took a deep breath and offered a thoughtful, measured response. "I don't believe what you're proposing was the intended purpose."

"My father died trying to rid this city of Big Jack and his ilk," Brent insisted. "I've been given a special gift. And now it's time I finally finished what he started."

"This is not how your father tried to accomplish it!" Worthington retorted. "I don't want you to meet the same end."

Brent filled another clip and slammed it down on the table. "This man took everything from me! He took my parents! He left me crippled! And it's because of him I lost Abbie."

"That may all be true," Worthington countered.

But Brent wasn't about to hear it. "There's no telling how many people he's killed. How many lives he's ruined. Tell me the city won't be better without him."

Worthington had no answer for that. "But I still believe there has to be a better way. The Good Book says, 'Thou shalt not kill.'"

"Yes," Brent added," and it also talks about standing up to evil, defending the defenseless, and especially not standing idly by while others suffer."

He loaded the final clip and wheeled himself around from behind the table.

Worthington felt a sudden chill as Brent closed his eyes for just a moment, then stood up from the chair. He stepped over to the older man, his lifelong caretaker, and looked him straight in the eye.

"I've been given a gift," Brent asserted firmly. "And now I intend to use it."

For the very first time, Worthington was actually intimidated by his young Master. Nevertheless, he stood his ground. Plus, he knew that Brent had never once been behind the wheel of a motor car.

"And if I refuse to drive you?"

"Then I will drive myself," Brent asserted.

VICKY slid into her sleek, new red dress. It was fancier and more expensive than anything she'd ever worn before. Much less something she actually owned.

She struggled to get it zipped up on her own. Then she made sure that everything had settled into the right spot. Especially after having downed all those milkshakes before landing in the hospital.

Finally, she stepped in front of the mirror. She had to admit it, she still cleaned up pretty well.

Except she wasn't used to showing so much cleavage. She grabbed the bust line and hiked it up further.

She'd asked for one with straps, but Vivian wouldn't hear of it. The dress was well-designed, but even so, Vicky was worried sick that something might slip out.

Otherwise, the dress fit perfectly, unlike her. Fit in, that is.

She still knew she'd stick out like a sore thumb next to all those blue blood gals and their thousand dollar frocks. Even wearing something that nice, how could she not? Spending half the night surrounded by the most beautiful and wealthiest women in Terminal City. She'd have given anything not to have to go.

Almost.

But Leonore had her over a barrel. She just couldn't do that to Brent Gregor. A man who'd already suffered so much in life.

And especially not after he'd helped her get on the crime beat. And save O'Donnell from the chair. And told Denny where to find her.

Even if he was a grade-A jerk to start with.

This was the price she paid for loyalty to a man she barely knew. But to whom she owed nearly everything.

LOCKED in his room and out of sight, Brent readied himself for the night ahead. The room was filled with an unsettling chill as he fastened the dual shoulder holster beneath his black suit jacket. He'd filled multiple clips and stuffed them into the pockets.

Finally, he opened the ornate, weathered red box given to him just weeks earlier by the old gypsy woman. He stared at its contents for the longest moment. Inside was the mask, hat, and cloak of The Black Spectre.

He'd only worn it once before. The night he somehow managed to rescue Vicky Rose from the Asylum. Which was also the very night he'd unexpectedly encountered Ned Vogel and quite nearly met his end.

This time it would be different, he thought.

Brent threw the cloak around his shoulders. He hadn't planned on wearing the ensemble again. But considering what he was about to do, he needed to conceal his identity. It really was the perfect disguise. With it on, he was completely unrecognizable.

The ring on his finger glowed brightly. He could feel its strength fill every ounce of his being. But it would also reveal his presence in the shadows. He took out the pair of black gloves and put them on.

Then he lifted the black mask out of the box. He stared at the gleaming white half skull that adorned it. It had unnerved him the first time he saw it.

He hoped it would do that, and more, to Big Jack.

CHAPTER NINETEEN

VICKY slowed down as she drove into Lakeview Heights. Partly to once again take in the opulent splendor on display, but mostly because she dreaded where she was going. It really was a different world there. Hard to believe all the wealth and frivolity with so many people out of work and suffering. She'd even passed a Hooverville on the way.

She was sure most women would have been thrilled with this assignment. Spending the evening in a beautiful mansion (truth be told, she was actually excited about that part), rubbing elbows with the creme-de-la-creme. Leonore certainly was excited about all that, and more.

But Vicky would have much rather been at the grand opening of the Four Diamonds. Surrounded by cigarettes, whiskey, gambling tables, and the very real possibility of impending danger. Instead of lolly-gagging around in this fantasy world.

As she rounded the corner, she saw the Gregor Mansion up ahead. She had a fleeting thought of stopping by. Surely he'd be home. He most definitely wouldn't be at the soirée.

She wondered if he'd even be in the mood for a visitor. Likely not, she reasoned. Especially at this hour and from an unannounced visitor.

She pulled over to the curb at the Gregor Mansion anyway, not far from the entrance gate. If she went and talked to him then, she considered, she could most assuredly skip the party.

But she'd firmly dismissed that course of action already. Why on earth would she consider it now?

As she was playing this mental game of Round Robin, one of the Gregor's Security Guards took notice. She was so lost in her own thoughts, she hadn't even noticed that he'd walked to the car.

She reacted with a start when he leaned over and tapped on the glass. "Excuse me, ma'am, but you need to move on."

She quickly produced her press ID and played dumb. "I'm sorry, do you know where the Kennelly home is?"

"Just follow this road around, Miss," he directed her. "You can't miss it." He backed away to allow her room and motioned for her to drive off. But instead, she leaned her head out.

"I'm sorry, just one more question," she added. "I'm a friend of Mr. Gregor's. Vicky Rose. I've been here before."

She thought for a moment that he might recognize her and just wave her on through. But he didn't. "Would you happen to know if he's attending the Kennelly party?"

"No Miss, I wouldn't," he told her then backed away again.

Clearly it was time for her to move on.

WORTHINGTON pulled the car into a dark alley only a few blocks from the Four Diamonds. He was careful to select a location without a dead-end. Close enough to the club, but not so close that they would be noticed.

Brent turned to the weathered, red box on the seat beside him and took a deep breath. The task ahead was difficult to be sure, but all he had to do was think of the pain that Big Jack had brought to his life. From there, he found the strength to do what was needed.

His ring glowed brightly within his black gloves. A sudden chill befell the automobile.

Worthington, ever the voice of reason, was still not convinced. "Please, Sir," he implored, "I must beg you once more to reconsider."

Brent looked at him with calm assurance. His voice was the same, but his tone was entirely different. It was like another person spoke through his body.

"Worthington, I appreciate your concern. But there's no need to worry. No one will see. I'll be back in a few minutes. And then we'll go home."

There was no consideration of the repercussions afterwards.

"Of course, Sir," Worthington answered in resignation. He wanted so very much to believe him. He almost did.

Brent opened the box and stared for a moment at the mask. He carefully pulled it over his head, completely erasing his own features.

Finally, he put on the blood-red head scarf and wide brimmed, black hat. He was no longer himself anymore. He was one of many who'd worn them. He was one of many who would use the Spirit Force to battle for justice.

He was The Black Spectre.

AS SHE stood in the grand entrance hall of the sprawling Kennelly mansion, Vicky thought about the thousand different ways she could die in a place like that. Her immediate desire was to run around the whole house and soak in every ounce of opulence that surrounded her. It was newer, brighter, and more inviting than the Gregor Mansion. Full of priceless paintings and treasures. All rather designed to impress, like everything else in the estate.

If her host'd had any idea of the effect fine furnishings had on her, he would have gladly shown her upstairs. Truth be told, he would try anyway.

Vicky grabbed the front of her dress and tugged it up. She hadn't gotten two steps in before Leonore suddenly appeared. "Well, look who actually showed up."

Leonore looked her over for final approval. "I must say, somebody cleans up pretty well. I told you. That Vivian can work wonders." That was the closest Leonore would ever come to a compliment.

"Just following orders," Vicky acknowledged. "Don't make me regret it before I even get in the door."

"You know," Leonore reminded her, "you don't have to be here if you don't want to. The Gregor Mansion is just down the street. I'm sure you passed it on your way in. I'll even give you a hint. It's right next to the Wentworth estate."

"No, thanks," Vicky replied with a pained smile. "I think I'll stay here." It took everything she had not to say more.

"Suit yourself," Leonore sang cheerfully before heading off to join socialite Constance Van Broman and distant cousin Gloria Lamonte. "I believe the other wallflower is over that way."

Leonore pointed her towards the next room and to Louisa Crocetti, who sat by herself in the corner. And was the only other guest who didn't want to be there any more than she did.

THE BLACK SPECTRE passed through the shadowy streets on his way to the Four Diamonds. With each step, he found himself grow stronger and more self-assured.

What's more, he discovered that he could move without making footsteps. It was a bizarre sensation that took him by surprise. He walked just as he had before. He stepped like any other man. Only his feet seemed not to touch the ground.

He had memories of floating in the air. Of stepping from a tiled roof and drifting to the ground. Memories that weren't his own.

He was tempted to try it. There were plenty of fire escapes nearby.

But it would have to wait. He was on a mission. He had a job to do.

One that would make the city a better place.

VICKY felt her headache come back, and it wasn't just because of Leonore. She was overdue for another dose and retreated to the fireplace (which was as big as her apartment) in the next room. It was the one quiet spot she could easily find.

She wasn't alone very long. Julius Kennelly immediately zeroed in on her, scotch in hand. He'd already had a few too many. It was if he could sense the addition of fresh pheromones in the air.

"What are those?" he asked with a lascivious smile.

"Headache pills," she replied, then grabbed his scotch

and tossed them back.

"Headache pills," he repeated with a knowing chuckle. "So what's your name, Sweetheart?"

"Rebecca," she told him. "Rebecca Randall."

"I've seen you before." He nodded with approval as he followed her every curve. "Come on, don't I know you from somewhere?"

She blushed demurely and instinctively put a hand over her heart. "Well, we're not too far from here, just on the outskirts of town.

"Oh, really?" he took the bait with a hungry grin.

"Maybe you've heard of it? We live on Sunnybrook Farm."

It took him a minute to get it. Actually much longer. But what he understood right away was that he wasn't about to get anywhere with her.

"Nice to meet you, Mr. Kennelly," she told him. "Please tell your wife she has a lovely home."

He turned around to find Margeaux standing in the doorway. With a very disapproving look. Julius just shrugged with a sheepish smile.

Vicky figured she must be getting used to that look. And probably not used to women turning him down. It didn't make Margeaux any friendlier towards her.

That was okay. She wasn't there to make friends.

THE SPECTRE reached the rear of The Four Diamonds. He immediately wished he'd had time to surveil the place beforehand. Just as Worthington had suggested. The entire building was lit up from the inside. Jazz music spilled out into the streets from every door and upstairs window. It was the perfect opportunity. Just as *he* had suggested.

There were only two guards at the back entrance. Both of them were drinking and complaining that they had to watch the door while everyone else was inside having a good time.

The Spectre reached for his gun, but then thought the better of it. Instead, he had to take them out quietly. Compared to those burly orderlies at the Asylum, this was a piece of cake.

He could have easily taken both of them down with just

two bullets. But despite the loudness of the festivities, someone would likely have heard.

When he pulled the trigger, he realized, his pistol should be aimed at Big Jack.

CHAPTER TWENTY

LOUISA CROCETTI didn't exactly look like a Mobster's daughter. Easily one of the prettiest young women there, she didn't look like a wallflower, either. She was meek and delicate, the picture of elegance and gentility. She'd endured many years of poise and etiquette training, and it showed in her every move. It also showed in her eloquence and cultured articulation.

But she didn't exactly look like a society maiden, either. Even in her classic and perfectly tailored gown, there was no mistaking her dark hair, dark eyes, and olive complexion. Due to her obvious heritage, she sat alone as always. Vicky had to wonder why a girl like Louisa would constantly subject herself to these things.

Vicky sat down next to the girl and offered a friendly ear. As someone who routinely lied to get to a story, this time she thought she'd try a novel tactic. Actually telling the truth. She figured that in order to converse with this young woman, she'd have to be completely honest.

Vicky quickly introduced herself to a confused Louisa. "Hi, Vicky Rose, with the *Daily Crusader*. Mind if I join you?"

Louisa was about to respond, but opted to back away instead. She knew the name (thank to the radio broadcast of the medal ceremony, who didn't?) and she also knew to be cautious. And rightfully so.

"Don't worry," Vicky reassured her. "I'm not here to dig up any dirt on your father. Actually, I want to talk to you."

This didn't make Louisa feel any better. "Please, just leave me alone."

BIG JACK proudly led Salvatore Crocetti into the ground floor saloon, excited to show off his new creation. The establishment was filled with revelers, most of whom were crowded around the bar. The bar itself covered the entire back wall, with every kind of booze imaginable. Three bartenders worked feverishly to fill the never-ending orders.

Vito Spats dutifully followed, as both bodyguard and host. He was constantly on the lookout for anything out of sorts. And was ready to quickly step in if need be. In particular, any of the news hounds that were enjoying the free opening night hooch. Like those two louses from *The Standard* who were already guzzling their fill like pigs at a trough.

Or, most especially, if any North Siders got the idea to try something while Big Jack and his crew had their guard down.

Behind Spats were Jack and Sal's beautiful young mistresses. Estelle Mercer, who'd played a large part in selecting the wallpaper and furnishings, explained the pineapple motif to Crocetti's mistress, chorus girl Cecelia Douras.

"So, this is where all my money went," Crocetti admired. "I have to say, Jack, it was money well spent."

"The silent partner finally speaks up!" Big Jack laughed heartily. "Just wait till you see upstairs!"

LOUISA was just about to rush off and find another corner in which to hide, when Vicky tried a completely different tactic. She reintroduced herself, only this time in broken Italian. And by throwing in every phrase she could remember.

"Mi scusi mille, per favore," Vicky struggled over every word. "Mi chiamo Victoria Rose. Sono da Gibsonville, Missouri. Vorrei solo essere amica." Though her uncertainty made it sound more like a question.

This at least made Louisa stop. This was the language

she heard spoken at home. Through which she conversed with her parents and family. This was the language with which she associated honest conversation.

The challenge was that Vicky didn't speak it very well. Or really much at all. As a former schoolteacher, she'd taught basic French, and had already forgotten much of it. But with the heavy presence of the Mob in Terminal City, she'd decided to tackle Italian. Thus far she was only versed enough to know basic vocabulary.

"Grazie mille," Louisa replied. "Mi dispiace, credevo che tu volessi parlare con me solo a causa di mio padre."

Vicky had to stop and repeat the words over in her head. She understood enough to get the gist. Especially the part about Louisa's father. That part she got loud and clear.

She asked her to repeat it more slowly. "Lentamente, per favore?"

Louisa offered her a friendly smile and did just that. Only this time in English. "My apologies. I assumed you only wanted to talk to me because of my father." Then she added, "Your pronunciation isn't bad."

"It's a lot better than my French, believe me," Vicky confessed.

"A lot better than my French, too," Louisa added as she warmed up to her even more. Out of all the soirées she'd attended, this was the first time anyone had ever tried to talk to her. And in her own language no less.

"How long have you been learning?" Louisa asked.

"Only a few months," Vicky explained. "At this point, I'm much better at pointing at things. Soffitto, pavimento, tavolo, forchetta.... But the verbs are killing me."

"I could tell," Louisa smiled.

BIG JACK led Crocetti and the girls into the largest of the second floor gambling rooms. It was filled with roulette tables, craps, and blackjack. For nearly every customer there was a beautiful young girl providing drinks, cigarettes, cigars, and more. All to happily provide whatever his customers desired.

Upstairs Spats was able to relax a bit. They didn't let just anyone on the higher floors.

Here, the clientele was much more exclusive. Chief LaSalle and Mayor Barker both played blackjack at the same table. With them was the handsome and friendly Albert Ronga who had a talent for finding beautiful women. A pretty young girl named Susan nuzzled up to Chief LaSalle and wore his hat. He'd promised to put her in handcuffs later.

Cecelia Douras gave Crocetti a playful tug on his sleeve. "So many beautiful girls here. Don't you think so, Darling?"

Crocetti leaned towards her with a mischievous look in his eye. "Pick out whichever one you like, Dear. We'll take her home with us."

Spats called for everyone to be quiet. "If I could have your attention, please. Big Jack would like to offer a toast."

Big Jack put an arm around Crocetti and raised a glass. "To my oldest friend and partner, a man who doesn't always want to be seen with the likes of me, but without whom none of this would be possible. Forever and always, my undying gratitude. Salute!"

VICKY eyed Louisa with incredulity as she tugged at her dress. She was immediately taken aback, astounded by what she'd just heard. "So, it's your *father* who's making you come to these things?" Just repeating the words out loud didn't make them sound any more believable. "Your mother had nothing to do with it?"

"I promise you, that's the absolute truth," Louisa assured her. "Mama's fought with him about it for years. She wants to teach me how to cook and change diapers. But Poppa's determined to have a son who's a senator and a daughter married to one."

And his efforts to turn the fair Louisa into a debutante was just one of the ways he'd intended to do it.

Saying it out loud didn't make it any more tolerable to Louisa, either. "Can you even imagine what that's like?"

Vicky could only nod her head in agreement. "Believe me, I do. My mother, my grandmother, my sister, they're all schoolteachers. My father practically disinherited me for becoming a reporter."

Vicky was surprised that, the longer she spoke to Louisa, the more she opened up about herself.

"That's a lot better than what my father would do," Louisa snickered.

Vicky burst out into a laugh. Loud enough that several people turned around to look at them.

She really liked this girl.

VITO SPATS was the first to notice the unnerving chill in the air. Not so much that the room had actually gotten colder (which it had), but that something wasn't *quite* right. He just couldn't put a finger on it.

He wasn't fast enough to do something about it. But he wasn't too slow to do nothing.

He turned around sharply and shoved Big Jack forward when the lights went out.

The room suddenly lit up with the bright flashes and loud cracks of gunfire. Screams filled the air as patrons and party girls all dove for the floor.

Big Jack caught a bullet in the shoulder. Another grazed his neck before he hit the carpet behind a blackjack table.

Willie, Fingers, Eggs, and the other men whipped out their guns.

And all fired back.

But not Spats.

He stood there motionless, lost in the briefest of seconds as bullets whizzed past him. He couldn't believe what he was seeing.

There, in the darkest corner, barely illuminated by the flashes of gunfire, was their assailant.

It was a figure dressed all in black.

As Spats strained to look in the darkness, he couldn't even tell if it was a man or a spectre. But there was one thing he could make out.

One detail he actually recognized.

The gleaming white skull on its mask.

And the sound of pain as the gangsters' bullets struck back.

CHAPTER TWENTY-ONE

Four Years Prior.

FOLLOWING graduation, Brent and Abbie began to drift apart. It was only natural, and should have been expected. She still had another year of school and spent most of her spare time flying.

Brent had come home to an emptier house than before. Nanny Miriam had already gone, of course, and so did some of the other staff. Worthington had hired a few new maids, like the red-headed one and the other girl.

Brent and Abbie did manage a handful of visits over the school year. He took the train back to Emerson for weekend visits. And, of course, she was home over the holidays. The last one, which had occurred in early Spring, was certainly the most memorable, and for a host of reasons. Not the least of which that it was also Abbie's first solo flight back to Terminal City.

Worthington and Abbie both feared that being idle would lead him into a pool of self-pity. And rightfully so. Neither knew just how correct that fear had been. With no need to work (he'd considered asking Uncle Dick about a job, but then quickly put the idea out of his mind) and no social calendar, Brent soon found himself with an abundance of time. And extremely idle hands.

Worthington repeatedly encouraged him to find something to occupy himself. He suggested law. It seemed ideal. Brent had long shown an interest in criminal justice, and he could follow in his father's footsteps.

Law school — perhaps even one near Emerson — seemed the ideal solution. But when Brent nixed that idea, Worthington had an even better one. He challenged Brent to pass the bar exam *without* going to law school.

It likely would have worked had Brent not become distracted by another subject. Medicine.

Once he'd gotten over his initial surprise, Worthington began to inquire about a suitable medical school. There were several excellent options both close to home and in New York.

But Brent had other ideas.

He was more interested in research. Specifically regarding spinal injury. He began to consult medical books and journals for all of the latest information and theories. He had Dr. Graves, his personal physician, spend a day on the estate to review the specifics of his injury, answer every single question, and weigh in on every theory.

Brent began to ponder the idea of finding a cure.

He reasoned that, if a cure were possible, he could achieve it. He certainly had the means to do so. Expense was not a concern.

If he could walk again, he also reasoned, he would no longer be stuck on the ground while Abbie found freedom in the skies.

He was open to any proposal.

WORTHINGTON bolted from the front door and raced across the drive, his arms flailing. Right behind him was Mr. Coleman who, though excited, was decidedly less hysterical. The sun was going down and the only sound anyone could hear was the roar of the airplane's engine.

Brent watched from the window as Worthington shouted at the top of his lungs. Though no one, not even Mr. Coleman, could hear a word. It was the only time in his entire life that Brent saw him lose his composure. Including that dreadful Halloween night years earlier.

Much to everyone's shock (the neighbors included) Abbie's plane crossed over part of her own family's property, narrowly avoided several trees, and clipped the top of the hedges that separated their estates.

Worthington and Mr. Coleman both had to do a quick about-face. They ran back towards the house as Abbie swooped down and set her biplane down on the front lawn. She had written the week prior to tell him that she was coming home, and that there was no need to pick her up at the train station. But she hadn't explained why.

Brent made it down to the foyer just in time to see Abbie come in with a still clearly distraught Worthington. Followed by a very impressed Mr. Coleman.

Dressed in her aviator jacket, leather helmet, goggles, and long, white scarf, Abbie was a very long way from the young girl in the pink dress who'd tormented Brent all those years ago.

"You all right, Mr. Worthington?" she asked him.

"Yes, of course," he stuttered, still breathless. "I just need to sit down and collect myself. Then young lady, you and I shall have a *long* talk."

Abbie was unfazed. As Brent well knew, she'd developed a bit of a rebellious streak.

Mr. Coleman echoed Brent's own thoughts when he let out a long whistle. "How in the world did you manage to set that thing down?"

"Was a little trickier than I thought it would be," Abbie gushed proudly. "Had to cut across our property and come in at an angle. Might have to use part of the road to take off again."

The rest of the weekend was just as eventful. Though in decidedly different ways.

EDWARD MORRIS, the Maitre d' at Vicedomini's, lead the young couple to Brent's preferred table. Abbie never cared for it, for the same reasons that Brent found it ideal. It was largely private and situated in the back. But because it made him more comfortable, she'd appeased him.

The day had not gone entirely well. Even Worthington could sense that an unspoken tension had developed between them. Abbie missed the hustle and bustle of the city and wanted to get out. She suggested that they go see a show and stay over in the apartment.

As expected, Brent was opposed to the idea. He didn't like the way people stared at him, he explained.

"Let them stare!" Abbie suggested. "The more you go out, the more they'll get used to it."

"Easy for you to say," Brent countered. "You're not the one at whom they stare."

With Spring on the horizon, Abbie hadn't wanted to lunch inside (not even in the solarium). So Brent gave in and requested their meal in the lakeside gazebo. Where they could relax in the lounge chairs, enjoy the warm breeze, and watch the swans.

After lunch, Brent told her the latest on his search for a cure. "I've just heard about a surgeon who's made wonderful advancements in treating physical defects. He has a clinic in Vienna. We could finally have a normal life."

She rolled over and took his hand. "Brent, that sounds absolutely wonderful. But either way, we can still be happy."

The rest of the day was spent indoors. Playing cards in the solarium and discussing books in the library. By the time dinner approached, Abbie was dying to leave the house.

Brent finally gave in. But he wasn't at all happy about it. Which he made quite clear.

As expected, he'd encountered the usual stares as Mr. Morris led them to their table. He knew what they were thinking. He'd even heard it many times before. *What is she doing with him?*

Abbie grew in frustration. "Can't you just ignore it for once? I spent nearly four hours by myself cramped in a little plane just to get here!"

"No one asked you to!" he snapped. The other diners turned around to look at them.

Abbie looked back at him tearfully. "Brent, you're embarrassing me."

"Well, I'd hate to do that now, wouldn't I?" he barked. "Honestly, I can't think of anything worse."

He always made it about the chair.

She took a moment to collect her thoughts. "Brent, please...."

"Perhaps it would be better if you just went back to Emerson," he interrupted. "Then you don't have to worry about always being stuck on the ground with me."

She sat there for a moment and fumed at him. He glowered back angrily as tears welled up in her eyes.

And that's when she got up and walked out of his life. Both literally and figuratively.

LATER that night, Worthington checked in on Brent as he sat in bed and stared out the window. As always, he could see the lights from the Wentworth Mansion breaking through the trees.

"I don't know what happened at dinner to-night," Worthington commented. "But I implore you to go over there and apologize."

"Apologize for what?" Brent retorted.

"That's immaterial," Worthington explained. He walked around the bed and sat down with his young charge.

"I'll be the first to admit that I am no expert on the ways of the heart. But on this I am certain. If you don't, I daresay you may never get another chance."

The next morning, Brent was awakened by the engines of Abbie's plane. He could have easily reached for his bell and called for Worthington. But pride stayed his hand.

He just listened as she taxied out across the lawn and took off.

CHAPTER TWENTY-TWO

WORTHINGTON turned around with a jolt as The Black Spectre jerked open the back door of the car and collapsed into the rear seat. He was absolutely stunned by what he saw. The Spectre gripped himself tightly and crumpled over in agonizing pain. He was bleeding profusely.

Worthington froze.

The Spectre summoned what little strength he had left to shout at the older man.

"HURRY!"

Worthington had just gotten the car into gear when the first of the gunshots shattered the rear glass.

He instinctively ducked down and slammed his foot on the gas pedal. A barrage of gunfire rained down on them. His heart nearly stopped from the sudden realization.

That was a Tommy gun.

Worthington managed to speed out of the alley and turn onto the nearest street as even more bullets ripped the right side of the car and shattered the windows.

He gunned the motor and drove as fast as he could for blocks on end, constantly watching his rear view mirror. He turned down one street and then another in desperate hope of survival.

After a few more turns and no more gunfire, he felt like they might have reached safety. But there was no way of knowing for how long.

Surely, the Mob would come looking for them.

And they wouldn't be far behind.

Worthington quickly pulled over to the curb and looked back at Master Gregor. Blood was everywhere. He couldn't imagine how Brent could survive.

"I need to get you to a hospital," Worthington stammered, trying to think of the closest one. Exceedingly worried that it might be a wasted effort.

"They'll find me there," Brent struggled.

Sadly, Worthington realized, that was true. Taking him to a hospital would be a sure death sentence.

His mind raced, trying desperately to find a solution. He had to do something. But what?

Then the thought struck him.

"Chinatown," he determined. "I know someone who might be able to help."

Worthington gave a quick look around and put the car back into gear. It was their only chance.

They knew how to keep secrets there. And it was the only place Big Jack might not be able to reach.

BIG JACK fumed as he picked himself up off the floor. Blood ran down the side of his head from where the first bullet had just grazed his neck. He clutched his bleeding shoulder where a second bullet had found its mark.

Jack grabbed the nearest tray of poker chips and threw them across the room. He was far more angry than injured. He wasn't as young as he used to be, but he'd suffered much worse.

He just couldn't believe someone would come into his place of business, at his grand opening no less, with all his guests of honor there, and take a shot at him.

Big Jack commanded Spats, "You find out who the son-of-bitch was took a shot at me! And you find out who sent him!"

"You got it, Boss," Vito Spats reassured him. "I'm thinking we put a few rounds in him. Fingers and Eggs went after him. He won't get far."

Spats had a pretty good idea of where to start.

Big Jack clutched Spats' shirt with a giant, bloody paw. "You put your ear to the ground, see what he can find out. This guy didn't just pop up out of nowhere."

Spats dutifully agreed. But he also knew something else. This wouldn't have happened in the old days.

For all his bluster, Big Jack was getting weak. And somebody else out there knew it.

LEONORE threw her head back and laughed with a hungry look in her eyes that said plenty. Julius Kennelly could be very charming when he was drunk. What was more, she was standing right there with her cousin, Gloria, and the gorgeous Constance Van Broman. And yet his eyes were firmly on her. She didn't want this night to end. At least not downstairs.

She especially didn't mind at all where his hand was. After all, she'd been the one to put it there. And becoming his latest conquest would go a long way to secure her position among the city's elite. She lived for nights like this.

Julius was just about to nuzzle up to her when he suddenly stopped. She looked up to see that his expression had immediately dropped.

"Maybe later, Sweetheart," he slurred and just as quickly sauntered off to his next conquest.

Leonore turned around and expected to see Margeaux. Instead, it was Vicky.

She crossed her arms and looked at her disdainfully. "What're you doing in here?" Leonore snapped.

Vicky wasn't sure she liked being the local killjoy. But in this instance it had worked in her favor.

Gloria, however, offered Vicky an inviting smile. "Leonore, who's your friend?"

"Not a friend. Just somebody from work," she grumbled.

"I'm leaving," Vicky informed her.

"What? So early?" Leonore asked with mock surprise. She glanced over to see that the wallflower corner was empty. "Getting past your bedtime? You and your little friend were getting along so swimmingly. Looks to me like you two speak the same language."

Gloria and Constance could barely suppress their giggles.

"My house has a curfew, what can I say?" Vicky told her. "Anyway, I'll have it on your desk first thing in the morning."

"Have what?" Leonore looked back at her puzzled.

"My story," Vicky told her emphatically.

"Oh right, of course," Leonore replied with mock interest.

CHARLIE HECHT and Ben Gelbart ducked into the rear stairwell of the Four Diamonds and looked around. There was just the steps going up, a narrow hallway leading back to the front, and a door leading outside. Probably to the alley behind the club.

They'd still been in the ground floor saloon when the shooting started. They knew that Big Jack, Salvatore Crocetti, Chief LaSalle, and even Mayor Barker were all up there. No telling who might have been injured.

They heard multiple footsteps overhead and ducked back in the doorway they'd just come out of. While everyone else screamed for the front door (including that milquetoast reporter from *The Daily Crusader*, Perry Philips — even Charlie had to admit that the skirt had more guts), they'd managed to cut through the store room and end up there.

"I swear, some of it sounded like it was outside," Gelbart commented.

"Can you believe our luck, Bennie?" Charlie asked, grinning from ear-to-ear. "Talk about being in the right place."

"Only thing that could've made it any better is if one of us had taken a bullet!" Gelbart observed excitedly.

Charlie didn't exactly share the sentiment. "Yeah, right."

Gelbart stepped out from the doorway and peered up the steps. Somehow, some way, they needed to find their way to the second floor. Especially before there was any more shooting. "Anybody coming?" Charlie asked anxiously.

Gelbart took a few steps and looked further up. "No, I don't see anybody. Come on!"

Gelbart had just bounded up the stairs when the second floor door flew open. He suddenly found himself face-to-face with a contingent of uniformed police officers who marched down with LaSalle, Crocetti, Mayor Barker, and a few dames in tow.

Charlie managed to duck back into the office just in time. He'd seen two of the janes before. One of them kept time with Big Jack, and the younger one worked for him. The third gal he didn't know, but judging by the way she clung onto Sal Crocetti, he had a pretty good guess.

"What're you doing in here?" the Sergeant barked.

Gelbart did his best to play it cool. "Just trying to make sure the Mayor and the Chief are okay. Gentleman, do you have any comment on this terrible tragedy? What can you do to find whoever's responsible?"

"Get this news hound outta here!" LaSalle barked.

One of the large Bulls grabbed Gelbart by the arm and hustled him right down the hallway towards the front of the building.

"Aww, come on, fellas!" Gelbart implored. "I gotta story to write!"

Despite Gelbart's disappointment, he never said a word to betray his compatriot. Better to have one of them get the scoop than neither. Charlie would have done the same for him any day. No doubt.

Hecht watched from the doorway as the rest of the contingent went straight to the back door. Another of the Bulls cracked it open and checked outside. Several cars, including a handful of black and whites, waited out back. Seconds later, they were all gone. And more importantly, they were never there in the first place. By the time the morning papers hit the street, all three men would have rock-solid alibis.

With the coast finally clear, Charlie cautiously emerged from the doorway. He was just about to head upstairs when he noticed several drops of blood on the floor. None of those men looked to be bleeding. And Big Jack had been taken out the front to a waiting ambulance.

The trail led out the back way.

As much as he wanted to get upstairs where the action had been, Charlie knew to follow his gut. And his gut was telling him that the story had moved on. Out that back door. He cracked it just enough to peer outside. And couldn't believe what he saw.

Two goons stood guard outside. But that's not what grabbed his attention.

The entire back parking lot was littered with bullet

shells. *Dozens* of bullet shells. They glistened against the pavement like stars in the moonlight.

Bennie was right. The worst of it *did* happen outside.

Charlie was careful to stay quiet as two more goons joined the three that were already there. Most of them he recognized. Tommy Clams, Eggs Milano, and Fingers Scarrone. All of them big guns. And armed to the teeth.

And in his biggest stroke of luck yet, he could hear every word of their conversation.

"Who was that guy?" Tommy asked, still stunned by what had just gone down.

"Don't know," Fingers told him. "But Spats thinks it's the same guy from the Asylum."

"Did you see him?" Tommy asked anxiously.

"Just a glimpse," Fingers confessed. "Was dressed all in black. Had a mask with this skull on it."

What the hell? Charlie had to wonder.

VICKY took a moment to again drive past the Gregor Mansion. She checked her watch. It was still certainly early enough. The lights were on and the grand house looked very much alive. But with Brent Gregor's understandable penchant for security, there was every possibility that he kept them on all night.

It pained her to think about him going all the way to California, only to find out that the love of his life, Abigail Wentworth, had gotten married. Vicky could only imagine the pain he must have felt.

It bothered her even more that she knew about it. And that she'd heard about it from Leonore.

People should be allowed to keep their own secrets, she thought. Even the rich and powerful.

And yes, she truly believed that, even as a reporter. Yes, it was her job to uncover the truth and to keep people informed. But this wasn't the news. This was his personal life.

She was really tempted to stop. Maybe offer a friendly ear? True, she didn't really know him. But he had helped her save a man's life. And according to Denny, he'd played a small part in helping her get rescued from the Asylum.

She felt it was the least she could do.

But if she were to stop (assuming she could even get past the guards at the gate), then she'd have to tell him why she'd done so. And she was pretty sure that wouldn't go over very well. Probably about as well as their first encounter. When she'd posed as his nurse. That was not an event she wanted to repeat.

As she put the car in gear and steered in the direction of home, she had to wonder about The Four Diamonds. Perhaps she'd been wrong. Perhaps the grand opening had been event-free.

She could only hope.

WORTHINGTON watched helplessly, aiding in whatever little way he could, as Father Antonio Pacelli and Sister Ruth worked feverishly to stop the bleeding. It looked very much like a hopeless cause, but a quick prayer to St. Jude gave them the will to do their best.

Father Pacelli was a gentle man who's thinning white hair and paunchy midsection gave evidence of how many years he'd served the Lord. He'd founded the Chinatown Parish almost ten years earlier, where Worthington had volunteered much of his time (and a fair sum of Brent Gregor's money) since Master Gregor had left for college.

Sister Ruth was a kind, but steadfast woman who'd assisted in starting the Parish and managed much of its day-to-day operation. Including the younger nuns who rotated through every year or so.

Thankfully, both she and Father Pacelli had some degree of medical training. She as a hospital nurse and he as an assistant to the medics during the Great War. He'd given far too many last rites during those days and was prepared to do everything he could to keep from having to do so again.

But almost as importantly, Worthington knew that they could be trusted. As soon as they pulled off the mask, they immediately recognized their patient.

The Black Spectre had fallen unconscious long before Worthington had pulled into the alley. Well out of sight of any prying eyes. Despite their shocked reaction, they'd helped Worthington carry him inside and lay him down on the table in the back room.

The Parish was a small collection of spare rooms. The largest was in the front (it opened to LaMonte Avenue, which ran the length of Chinatown) and was used for worship services. The few smaller rooms were used for the Parish office and a prayer room. The back room was primarily a kitchen or, as on this night, used for whatever else may be required.

Once they had their patient stabilized, Father Pacelli was able to turn to the many other matters at hand.

He instructed Sister Ruth, "Call Dr. Tung. Tell him to come right away."

Just before she rushed out, he added, "And then call Yo Hing. He'll know what to do with the car."

"Do you think he'll live, Father?" Worthington asked in desperation. He was nearly unable to get the words out.

"I wish I could say," Father Pacelli replied. "He's in God's hands now."

EPILOGUE

DETECTIVE SHAYNE carefully surveilled the back alley behind the Four Diamonds. The pavement was littered with spent shells. He picked one up. If he had to guess, just based on the sheer number, he'd say it came from a Tommy gun. Likely more than one.

He followed the shells out of the alley. The trail led down a narrow side street for another full block. Then to a second alley. There he found shattered glass scattered all about. Most likely from a car window. The rear window. And tire tracks leading out the other side. And many, many more shells.

This was where the assassin had made his get-away.

Shayne scratched the stubble on his chin. Something puzzled him.

He didn't see any evidence of where the assassin had fired back. This wasn't a Mob shoot out. This was an escape.

Whoever'd taken a shot at Big Jack had tried to run. And taken a few bullets himself in the process.

He was sure the Mob was already combing the nearby hospitals. Chances were this guy was already dead. But if he did manage to survive, then one thing was perfectly clear.

There was a new player in Terminal City.

WORTHINGTON found it better to wait in the tiny prayer room. It was a simple, confined space with the same white walls as the rest of the Parish. The only furnishings were a few chairs and an old dresser used as an altar.

Worthington lit a candle next to the crucifix and fell to his knees.

Despite the passage of time, the sting was all-too familiar. He was flooded with terrible memories of that fateful night fifteen years prior. When he'd cradled young Brent tightly, his hands pressed into the bullet wounds, doing his level best to stem the bleeding. Trying desperately to keep the child alive until Dr. Wellman and the ambulance could arrive.

He begged then that the Heavenly Father might see fit to let Master Gregor live. Just as he did now. As before, he well knew that it would only be by God's will.

This time, however, the situation was far more dire. Not only were his injuries far greater, but there were men combing the city right then, looking to finish the job. Which precluded them from the appropriate medical care.

Thankfully, Father Pacelli had taken them in. Even more thankfully, Dr. Tung had arrived less than five minutes after Sister Ruth's call. He'd wasted no time on pleasantries and had immediately gone to work on his new patient. Short of going to a hospital, Master Gregor was in the best of hands. And their presence safely unknown.

With his knees growing weak, Worthington struggled back to his feet and sat down in a chair. He prayed again and again for God's mercy.

He was soon joined by Sister Amelia, a young nun in training who'd only been with the Parish a short time. She sat down next to him and took his hand.

"I thought you might like some company," she offered. "Two voices are always stronger than one."

VICKY unlocked the outside door of her building and pushed it slowly, trying her best to keep the squeaking to a minimum. She opened it just enough to squeeze through. It was nearly past curfew and the last thing she'd wanted to do was wake Mrs. Hershey. She'd even taken her shoes off so as not to make a sound.

She'd just gotten to the stairs when the older woman opened her door and looked on disapprovingly. Almost made it. But more than likely not. Mrs. Hershey had probably been watching from her window when Vicky drove up.

"Miss Rose," the elder landlady barked quietly but firmly. "It's nearly past curfew, you know."

"Yes, I'm aware, Mrs. Hershey. Which is why I arrived *before* curfew."

"Only just," Mrs. Hershey corrected her. Then out of the blue she added, "My but that's a lovely dress you have on." Vicky wasn't sure if this was a compliment or just a springboard to further chastisement.

After a few seconds of silence, Vicky realized that it must've been the former. How odd, she thought. The older woman rarely had a kind word to say.

"Thank you," Vicky replied, still a bit confused as to whether or not that was the proper response.

"I say," Mrs. Hershey continued, waving a couple of pink note pages as Vicky went up another two steps. "I wouldn't have stopped you at this late hour, but you've had another urgent message from your sister."

Vicky had to stop short on that one. *Must be serious for Liz to call twice in one week*, she thought. And it was urgent. Or was Mrs. Hershey just exaggerating?

She had to wonder, was this the inevitable call? The one where she found out that her estranged father, who'd had one foot in the grave all these years, was finally on his deathbed? Or worse yet, had actually passed away?

Vicky quickly glanced at her watch. She felt like she should call Liz back. But it was a "school night" and really much too late. That was as good an excuse as any to not face the inevitable.

"Thank you, Mrs. Hershey," Vicky said before starting up the stairs yet again. She'd nearly made it up to the second floor before the landlady stopped her once more.

"Miss Rose," Mrs. Hershey said firmly. "You also have a message from a gentleman caller. He's telephoned several times."

That Denny. What on earth could this be about, she wondered? She just shook her head in frustration. This whole... boyfriend situation was not working out at all like she'd wanted.

"You really should explain to your male suitors that we have a curfew on the telephone as well," Mrs. Hershey continued.

"Oh, believe me," Vicky firmly reassured her. "I'm going to have a nice long talk with Denny to-morrow."

Vicky was about to clear the top landing when Mrs. Hershey stopped her yet again. "No, this was a Mr. Hecht."

"Charlie?" Vicky reacted with a start. "What'd he say?"

"He just said that it was urgent," stated Mrs. Hershey. "But as I was saying, I don't mind you having gentlemen callers. But you must abide by the rules, Miss Rose. We have a very strict curfew on visitors. And as I reminded you, that includes use of the telephone."

Vicky didn't hear a single word the older woman said. She was too busy trying to sort out why on earth Charlie Hecht would be calling her at home. Especially at this hour. Yes, there was the possibility that it was a social call. She wouldn't put it past him.

But surely, it had to be something else. Something important for him to try to reach her at this late hour. That likely meant he had to be working late. And if Charlie Hecht was working late, then something had gone down.

Something big.

Vicky hurried back down the steps and plucked the notes from the older woman's hands. Sure enough, the message from Liz just said "urgent" and nothing more.

The message from Charlie said the exact same thing. But with a return number. The number for *The Standard*.

Something had definitely gone down.

END.

READ THE NEXT EXCITING CHAPTER!

A masked hero fights for his life. An ailing reporter faces uncertain death. Will either live until morning?

Following his failed attempt to kill Big Jack, Brent Gregor (aka The Black Spectre) lies near death in a Chinatown parish. Determined to locate the mysterious assassin, the Mob combs the blood-soaked streets to find him. His only hope of survival lies in the mercy of strangers.

Furious that she missed out on the story of a lifetime, Vicky is stunned to learn that her mysterious savior is actually real. Ignoring Editor Frank Matson's orders and her own failing health, she goes after the story with a vengeance. But to get the answers she so desperately needs, she will have to march straight into the lion's den. Alone.

READ THE FIRST EXCITING CHAPTER!

An ambitious reporter looking for her big break. A millionaire recluse looking for a cure. Can they survive a violent, corrupt city?

Vicky Rose is a reporter stuck in the City Hall beat, but she knows she's destined to cover crime. She sees her chance at a big break when the mayor is murdered in his office.

Reclusive millionaire Brent Gregor has been trapped in a wheelchair since the night a home intruder killed his father. Now, the only thing he cares about is being able to walk again.

The mayor's murder reeks of mob violence, but all the evidence points to someone else. Vicky knows the only hope of finding the truth rests in Gregor's hands, but he's unwilling to help until the one person who might be able to cure him changes his mind....

www.blackhoodpress.com

About the Author

Roger Alford grew up on a steady diet of *Star Wars* and Jim Henson. After discovering old time radio and movie serials in college, he realized he'd been born in the wrong decade. His Internet videos, which include the popular mash-ups *The Twilight Zone: Planet of the Apes* and *Raiders of the Lost Ark: The Serial*, have been featured on ABC News, CNN, Inside Edition, plus multiple books and newspapers. When he's not plotting the latest adventures of The Black Spectre or brushing up on Mafia history, he's traveling the country and eating in great restaurants with his wife and family.

GYPSY: 2-5-12-8-5-24 18-10-21-7-21-9-21-24
25-4-9-9 7-21-12-5-26-21 10 19-10-16-4

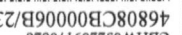